# Maverick Gun

# MAVERICK GUN

## LEE MARTIN

### AVALON BOOKS
THOMAS BOUREGY AND COMPANY, INC.
401 LAFAYETTE STREET
NEW YORK, NEW YORK 10003

PRINTED IN THE UNITED STATES OF AMERICA
ON ACID-FREE PAPER
BY HADDON CRAFTSMEN, SCRANTON, PENNSYLVANIA

To James Liontas, founder of Peninsula University Law School, my alma mater. Jim is a true maverick, whose daring and fearless determination have made him a success in every endeavor. In the spirit of the Old West, an obstacle to Jim is a challenge and another opportunity.

## Chapter One

As he rode into Shotgun Wells in western Montana Territory in the spring of 1881, his wide-brimmed Stetson shading his dark-brown eyes and slightly crooked nose, Wes Carson rested his cold right hand on his Army Colt. Haney, the foreman of the Little River H, rode at his side. He had hunted Wes down at the Powder River, and Wes had come because Angela Hollis had sent for him.

The streets were muddy, and Wes's buckskin stallion carefully made its way, as if stepping to the jingle of Wes's silver spurs. The men were hot and dusty from the trail, their weary thoughts suddenly interrupted.

A young woman was being pulled from the saddle on her black mare by a big husky, mean-eyed rowdy. Even as she struck at him with her fists, he was dragging her down into his arms. Another, smaller, man stood aside, grinning.

On the boardwalk on both sides of the near-empty street, men and women stared. No one moved to help. Even the angry-faced men in front of the saloon would not come forward, fear written on their faces with frantic glances.

Her lustrous red hair flying about her face, she was fighting as the bigger man tried to kiss her, even as her riding skirts swept the mud. The younger man grabbed her arm as she kicked at him furiously.

"Settle down, Cindy." The bigger man laughed, still holding her. "You won't tell your Grandpa 'counta you know he'd get shot up for sure. We don't take much to squatters, anyhow. So come on, give old Sal a kiss."

For a brief moment, Wes hesitated.

"That's two of the Grubers you come here to fight," Haney muttered. "Sal's got his hands on Cindy Taylor. The smaller one, that's Seth."

Wes rode his buckskin forward. He was damp under his double-breasted shirt. He rubbed his cleft chin and pushed his Stetson higher on his brow. His big shoulders drew back as he grimaced.

Wes lifted the reins and slapped his stallion's rump, urging it forward, and it lunged between the two men, knocking Seth Gruber flat on his rear in the wet mud. Wes bent from the saddle to slam his fist down on the head of Sal Gruber. Stunned, the man staggered aside, Cindy freed from his grasp.

Wes reached down and slid his arm about the woman's waist, then swung her up to his side and onto the pommel against him. He spun his stallion about and headed for the boardwalk.

But he caught his breath as he gazed at her surprised grass-green eyes, the gorgeous face and rosy lips, the high cheekbones and peach-colored skin with freckles on her small nose. Her silken dark-red hair, the rich color of a Texas sunset, was moving about her face and throat. There was a tiny silver scar on her chin, and she smelled of sweet lilacs. She had to be in her mid-twenties, at least seven years younger than Wes, and there was no ring on her left hand as she gripped his shirt.

"Put me down," she whispered.

He heard a dog growling somewhere as she struggled to be free of him. He swung his mount and leaned to set her down on the boardwalk, but her skirt was caught on his spur. He had to shake and lift her to free the cloth. Then, finally, he set her on her feet.

Cindy was still staring up at him as he straightened in the saddle. Behind her, men and women were startled and wide-eyed. Some looked frightened. The women and most of the men disappeared into buildings.

"Be careful," the young woman said anxiously.

Wes turned in the saddle to look at the two row-dies. Both had recovered and were standing inches deep in the mud. Sal, who had grabbed the woman, was adjusting his gun belt. He looked in his mid-twenties. Seth, younger and with the same hawklike face, black mustache, and dark eyes, grabbed his arm.

"Let it go, Sal. He's a stranger."

"He's with Haney."

The sunlight danced on the rainwater still pock-eted in the mud. There was no wind that morning; the air was still and brisk. The crowd was deathly silent, women gone from sight, while the men backed away. Merchants looked nervous, but the cowhands and grizzled farmers were curious.

"Get off your horse, mister," Sal called.

"That's Sal Gruber," a man said from the crowd. "You'd better turn and ride, stranger. He'll shoot you down without blinkin' an eye. And he's plenty fast."

Wes swung slowly down from the saddle, his spurs jingling. He lifted the stirrup and took his time loosening the cinch. His stallion nosed his arm. Then Wes draped the reins around the hitching rail.

To his left, there were two sorrel horses tied fast, both with the Box G brand. Beyond was the rambling street of a typical cow town. A wagon stood empty in front of the general store on the right. Mules were lined up near the express office farther up and across the street, beyond the jailhouse. Wolf pelts hung outside the saddle shop near the hotel, which was in front of him.

Suddenly, a small, fuzzy white dog with black hair over its eyes and black whiskers charged out of the alley and started to bite at Wes's boot. It was snarling and biting, and now it had its teeth clamped on Wes's britches at the ankle.

The crowd burst out laughing, and a rough-looking man in a leather apron, who appeared to be the local blacksmith, came forward. ''He's a stray mongrel we been feedin'. But just now he come out of the alley and started growlin' when you was car-ryin' Miss Taylor on your horse.''

Wes shook his boot, but the dog wouldn't let go.

The blacksmith reached down and grabbed the dog by the nape of the neck. It snarled and barked as it was pulled away, its little blue eyes still angry. The laughter subsided, and silence returned, broken sud-denly by Sal Gruber's cold voice.

''Turn around, mister.''

Wes drew a deep, silent breath. He knew his Colt was well oiled and loaded in his cut-down holster. Not being afraid to die had made him a fearsome opponent, but now he had to stay alive, had to see Angela.

Slowly, he turned to see the two rowdies still in the middle of the street. He moved deliberately away from his horse and out into the mud, his boots sinking deep. The sun was warm and high above. The hush from the crowd carried its own breathless sound.

Sal Gruber was standing with feet apart, his hand near his six-gun. His younger brother moved away toward the boardwalk, while trying to stop the fight.

"Sal, come on, we had our fun. Let's go on home."

"Nobody roughs up a Gruber and gets away with it."

"Pa don't want no town trouble."

But Sal Gruber ignored him.

Wes moved into the street, making sure any wild shots that missed him would head harmlessly past his horse and the crowd on the boardwalks.

Across the street, he saw two other punchers in front of the café. Faces were at the windows. Above the food store, the door to the doctor's office was open, and a small man leaned on the railing to watch. Everyone was waiting to see who was going to be killed.

Sal Gruber spread his feet farther apart. "All right, mister, make your play." His voice was high-strung, persistent. He was swaggering, bursting with pride and power and burning with anger. Color flushed his rough face. "Come on. I'll show you what happens when you cross a Gruber around here. But I like to know a man's name afore I kill 'im."

Haney, still on his bay, leaned on the pommel. "His name is Wes Carson."

Sal sneered, eyes narrowed. "Well, now, the fancy gun from Powder River. Don't scare me none. Fancy men die just as easy."

Wes felt sweat trickling down his back. Everyone had watched while the youth had manhandled a young woman, and no one had stopped him. They were all afraid. And now it was obvious that Wes's name had only whetted the man's appetite.

"Scared, huh?" Sal called. "Well, see this here silver dollar? When it hits the ground, you'd better draw, 'cause I'm gonna kill you dead."

There was no sign of the law. The quiet little town was so hushed, Wes could hear the coin flip from Sal's hand.

Now the silver dollar spun in the air, catching the sunlight as if it were a falling star. It came crazily downward, seeming to take forever, a glistening circle that spiraled toward the mud, a gunman's trick to make the other man draw.

The frightened citizens of Shotgun Wells watched the two men as the silver dollar headed for the mud.

As it landed, Wes drew with lightning speed, his hand moving faster than a rattler's head, so fast no one had seen it move. There was a gasp from the crowd.

And Sal Gruber, his six-gun out of his holster but not leveled, turned gray, his dark eyes round with surprise and dread. He was staring at the barrel of Wes's Colt, knowing he could die any second. Worse, he had been shamed in front of the town.

Seth, anxious, stepped forward from the board-walk.

There was a hush that held the crowd in its grasp, and Wes stood quiet, his six-gun aimed at Sal's gut. Shame set color racing through Sal's face, and bravado flushed over the shame. Slowly Wes lowered his weapon but didn't holster it.

Suddenly, as if thinking he had Wes fooled, Sal jerked up his six-gun and fired. Wes was forced to fire back. Sal's bullet went wild, whistling past Wes's ear.

But Wes's bullet hit the man dead center in the chest. Sal gasped and staggered forward from the impact. Eyes wild, he dropped to his knees, firing into the dirt. Then he fell face-down into the mud.

Wes felt the same sickness in his belly that he experienced every time he had to kill a man. He bit his lip.

Seth ran forward and knelt, turning his brother over, but the man was dead. "Aw, Sal, why'd you have to go and do that, anyhow?" Tears in his eyes, he asked two men to help him put his brother on one of their sorrels.

Mounted, Seth turned to look at Wes. His voice was hoarse as he said, "You ain't heard the last of this, Carson. Just wait till my pa and brothers get back from Butte.''

Then he rode out of town with his brother's body, disappearing over a far hill before anyone could speak. The uneasy silence remained until Wes turned from the street, his silver spurs tinkling.

The little dog broke loose, charged through the mud, its belly dragging, and began snarling and biting at Wes's boot. Everyone laughed heartily, relieved that the fight was over and that comedy had returned.

Wes tried to shake the dog off again, and the blacksmith came out and grabbed it by the neck, hauling it back and holding it while it snarled and barked at Wes.

''Seems to me,'' the man said, ''you'd better keep your distance from Miss Taylor.''

''And,'' a fat merchant said, ''from the Grubers. My name's Churchill, son.''

Wes couldn't help but stare at Cindy Taylor. She was uncommonly beautiful, especially on the frontier where life was so hard on women. Her long hair was soft and glistening like the glow of red-hot coals. She was kneeling on the boardwalk now, fondling the little dog that licked her hands and whined.

Wes glanced at Haney, who stood away from them, watching. A weathered man with a white handlebar mustache, Haney was maybe sixty and with a lot of hard years, but his pale blue eyes misted as he watched the young woman with the animal.

"You look just like a Scotchman I knew once," Cindy mused aloud to the dog. "I'll call you Scotty."

Churchill cleared his throat. "Son, you're plenty fast all right, but them Grubers will be back looking for you, and they won't care about your reputation. They'll shoot up the town. Why did you come here, anyway?"

"I'm headin' for the Little River H."

Cindy's face lost all color. She got to her feet in dismay, anger flashing in her gaze. "You're a hired gun for Hollis?"

"I didn't say that."

Her color returned hot and deep as her fury rose. "Our ranch is squeezed in between Hollis and the Grubers. Two years ago we came out here from Missouri for a new life after my father died. My mother got sick. Our hands were all run off. Tryin' to do the work of three men, my grandfather was hurt by a horse—all because of Hollis and the Grubers."

Wes shrugged, listening to her tirade in silence.

"And now there's another gun in town," she said.

"And you're mighty ungrateful."

Her chin went out, her green eyes flashing. "I could handle those Grubers, anytime. But you'd better watch your back, Mr. Carson. They're going to kill you.''

With that, she strutted off, the dog at her heels. Wes watched her with some amusement, but he felt his own face burning from her tirade.

Churchill moved closer, wiping his brow. ''You and Haney had better go on out to Hollis's place. If you leave now, you'll get there before dark.''

''Where's the law around here, anyhow?'' Wes asked.

''The sheriff's out of town. Now look, mister, the Grubers could be back here before nightfall. I'd sure take it kindly if you moved on.''

''You in charge around here?''

''Well, I'm justice of the peace.''

Later, over steak and eggs at the nearest café, Haney began to fill Wes in on details. On the trail, they had talked mostly of the buffalo slaughter and everything except why Wes was so willing to come. Wes had wanted it that way, but now they were in Shotgun Wells and getting close to the ranch. Haney spoke wistfully.

''Mr. Hollis moved in north of the river a few years before Gruber and his four sons took over the south side. I was with Hollis from the beginnin'. Back then they both had Injuns to worry about, but as time went on and the town grew, they both started grabbin' all the grass and water they could. Then the Taylors moved in right between 'em, south of the river and right on land the Grubers have been claimin'."

"Sounds familiar."

"Then, like I said, a couple of months back, Hollis's oldest son, Randy, got murdered along the river, and no one can prove who done it. Hollis still has his son Reggie and Angela. And that Cliff Sellers who's courtin' her."

"But you said no date was set."

"No, and this is the third fellow she's been gonna marry since they come up here."

Wes was silent, afraid to hope it was because of him.

Haney leaned back. "Mr. Hollis is the best cowman I ever worked for. He knows cattle. The Little River H is the finest spread in this part of Montana Territory. And he ain't a-feared of nothin', but he's smart. He knows you gotta fight fire with fire. Fast guns don't respect nobody but their own kind. That's why he needs you. Angela asked you to come, but it's Mr. Hollis who'll make the deal."

"I'll talk to him, but I ain't promisin'."

"Mr. Hollis said you'd be holdin' some kind of grudge."

"You're darned right I am. Five years ago, the Hollis wagons pulled into Fort Apache when we was fightin' Victorio. But when I got serious, her Pa stepped in. He figured I was just a gunhand. Soon as things got safe, he hauled her off to Montana. She was the only woman I ever wanted to marry.''

''You were scoutin' for the Army then?''

''Yeah, but I reckon I already had some kind of reputation I didn't want, from down in Texas.''

''You got any family at all?''

Wes shook his head sadly. ''My folks and little sister died from yellow fever in Memphis, back in '78, while I was with the Army.''

''Sorry to hear that.''

''Got word three months later.''

Haney shrugged. ''But anyway, you got Victorio?''

''Yeah, but it was the Mexican army got him. That's when I come up to Cheyenne. Did some scoutin' at Fort Laramie for a while. That's the most wide-open fort I ever did see. It's a blamed good thing the Sioux had other things on their minds. After that, I got work with the stock growers. I chased rustlers and got most of 'em.''

''We heard you was roundin' 'em up.''

''But before long, I was down to huntin' cowboys who took a few mavericks. They were buyin' trail stragglers and even payin' grazin' fees, tryin' to get their own start. Now Sturgis wants to blacklist 'em.''

''Sturgis, he's in charge?''

Wes nodded. ''With too tight a rein. I reckon I was ready for a change.''

But it was more than that. When Haney had shown

up at Wes's campfire one night along the Powder River, it had been five years since Angela had rejected him. Wes still blamed her father, but when Haney had said she was asking for his help, Wes had not hesitated for a moment.

Haney downed his coffee. "Now, I figure anything you want, Mr. Hollis will give you, just to hire you on."

"What's the best piece of land he's got?"

"Why, that'd be Turkey Creek."

"If it's something he wants to keep, that's what I'm askin' for."

"Don't ever tell 'im I put you on to it."

"Don't worry. I didn't hear it from you."

They left the café and were heading for their horses when they saw Cindy Taylor in front of the general store. She was trying to tie down a large sack of flour on the back of her saddle. Her mare kept dancing and the flour slipped, again and again.

No one moved to help her. Wes could only watch a moment before he stepped off the boardwalk and approached. He saw the annoyance on her face, but there was curiosity in her eyes. She was not very good at pretending to be aloof, nor could she make her soft voice sharpen.

"I don't need any help."

"Maybe you just need some instruction."

"Not from the likes of you."

He caught up the reins of her mare as Cindy fell

back. With the left rein in his left hand, also gripping the cinch strap, he forced the mare to back up several steps and sideways until it was against the rail. With his right hand he shoved the sack in place and pulled the saddle strings around it. Leaning on the mare, he tied the sack down securely.

Then he turned to look at her. He had to grin, because her chin was jutting out with its little scar shining in the sunlight. Her eyes were glistening, her mouth fighting a smile, and she tried to sound tough.

"Get it through your thick head: I don't need your help."

"How'd you get that scar, anyhow?"

She flushed, taking the reins from him as the mare nosed her arm and side. "None of your business."

"Let me see that."

He reached for her chin, startling her and the mare. She backed away as he laughed. Her face reddening, she turned to mount. Once in the saddle, she glared down at him.

"Just who do you think you are?"

"I'm the man you're gonna invite to supper one night right soon."

"You're out of your mind." She hesitated a moment, staring down at him as if completely dismayed. A hesitant smile crossed her lips, and her eyes twinkled. Then she spun her mare about and headed out of town at a walk.

Wes waited, hoping she would turn around and look back. She didn't, and he was disappointed. Then he wondered why. He had just ridden over three hundred miles to see Angela Hollis. Maybe it was Cindy's red hair that fascinated him.

Haney came to stand at his side. "What was that all about?"

Wes shrugged, because he wasn't sure himself.

Riding north out of town, they found the sun bright as the cold wind rose around them. The rolling green hills spread before them as the buckskin stallion and chunky bay picked their steps through the mud and grass. From a rise, they looked down on the wandering blue of Little River, which ran west to east and bordered the southern range of the spread.

"Don't let that river fool you, Wes. When it rains, you can't get across. And looky there, some of the herd. Most of 'em are crossbreeds, you know. More meat on 'em, but they don't winter good."

After they forded the shallow spread of the busy river, there were cottonwood and aspen groves along the little creeks that fed it. Beyond were the black buttes. Cattle grazed everywhere, and some still had a great spread of horns, clanging now and then against an unfriendly companion.

Two cowhands were riding up the hill toward Wes and Haney. They were elderly men who sat their saddles as if they had never learned to walk. Both wore long handlebar mustaches and leather vests.

Their faces were weathered and lined, and their ban-
dannas were soiled from constant use. They reined
up, and one pushed a stained, battered hat away from
his brow.

"Haney, glad to see you're back."

"This here's Wes Carson."

"Mr. Hollis said you'd be comin'. You're the
man who catches rustlers. I'm Pete, and this here's
Barney."

Haney quickly told them about the gunfight and
how Wes had killed Sal Gruber fair and square.

The two men stared at Wes, and Pete took a chaw
of tobacco before asking, "You beat 'im to the
draw?"

Wes nodded, embarrassed at their sudden admiration. He shook their hands and rode on with Haney.
His reputation was growing out of proportion, and
he didn't like it.

Wes and Haney rode down to a singing creek,
then followed it to the hollow and the rise where the
ranch buildings stood. There were many corrals,
some on the flat, and a lot of hands working some
broncs.

On a rise was a grand old house, painted green,
elegant with columns and a grand porch. It had a
veranda that circled the upper floor with a white-
washed railing and flowerpots. They dismounted at
the railing in front of the house and walked up the
steps to the door, where Haney knocked.

Wes held his breath. Just the thought of seeing Angela was painful. She had been the first woman in his life and had left a bitter taste, yet he was certain he would fall all over himself when he saw her, and that was causing him anxiety.

An elderly Mexican woman, her face wrinkled and eyes gleaming, opened the door.

"Maria, is Mr. Hollis at home?"

"He comes now."

She closed the door on them. Wes wondered if Angela was watching from behind some window curtains. He and Haney walked back down to their horses and watched a distant rider approach.

The rancher was on a big roan. As he dismounted near them, Wes recognized Hollis's harsh, lined face with its red tint. He was a big man with reddish-brown hair that was graying like his thick mustache. He wore a leather coat and vest. His dark eyes were gleaming.

"Mr. Hollis," Haney said, "Wes Carson here just tangled with Sal Gruber."

"That so?"

"Sal called him out and had just cleared his holster, but he turned white as cotton. Wes had 'im cold, but he let him go. Then Sal tried to trick 'im and fired straight out, and Wes had to kill 'im."

Hollis stared at Wes a long moment, his dark gaze moving down to Wes's cut-down holster strapped to his thigh.

"Well, Carson, you ain't changed much since Fort Apache. But the word is you're the fastest man alive." Reed shoved his hat away from his lined brow. "I reckon the Grubers will be comin' after you, so you may as well be paid. And I got trouble. I guess you know about my son Randy bein' killed."

Both men glared at each other a long moment, Wes remembering the rejection and Hollis again considering him to be nothing more than a saddle tramp, paid killer, and gunman and nowhere near good enough for Angela. But the rancher eased off and spoke grimly.

"Maybe while you're here, you can sniff out who done it. And maybe you can figure out who the rustlers are what killed old Joe, one of my best hands, and took maybe twenty head, up at Turkey Creek."

Wes pushed his hat back, his anger at this man flashing in his dark eyes, his cleft chin jutting forward. Hollis continued, his voice deepening as he saw the ire and tight restraint in Wes's gaze.

"Grubers and their gunmen been harassing my men in town and on the trail. They keep pushing to see how much they can get away with, and they coulda done the killings. That's why my foreman went to find you."

"To do what?" Wes asked.

"To stand up to the Grubers. I figure your name is worth their speed and all the hired guns they got.

I've fourteen men, but they're not gunhands. And I know you don't scare easy and you don't back off. So your bein' here will make 'em tread more carefully around the Little River H.''

"Let me tell you straight out, Mr. Hollis. I don't kill a man unless it's in a fair fight. If I work for you at all, it's to get my own spread.''

Wes stood firm, his sense of justice demanding that this man pay plenty for having kept Angela from him.

The rancher thought a long moment, his gaze fixed on Wes as he hesitated. Then he leaned on his roan, his eyes narrowed but his manner a little more friendly, as he appeared to respect Wes's desire to own a piece of land.

"I'll make you a deal, Carson. Five hundred now. When it's over, a section and fifty cows with a bull. And another five hundred. But you keep a tight rein until somethin' explodes. Agreed?''

"Who'll say when it's over?''

"It'll be over when the rustlin' stops and if a year goes by with no killin'. Now what about the deal?''

"Make half of 'em heifers, the rest young cows that have been proven, and guarantee the bull. And I pick the section. But I'll take a deed instead of the first five hundred.''

Hollis hesitated, studying Wes and taking his measure.

## Chapter Two

Standing in front of the Hollis ranch house with Haney and facing Hollis, Wes had made his demand as tough as possible. He could see the fury in Hollis's face. The rancher cleared his throat, his dark eyes burning.

"All right, Carson, but you'd better be good."

"What's more, I was talkin' to some of your men, and it seems the section I want is called Turkey Creek Meadows."

Fury flashed color across Hollis's face. He swallowed hard, eyes burning. "I was tryin' to hold that canyon, but I had to pull the herd back 'counta rustlers. That's where Joe was shot in the back."

"So it ain't no use to you."

Hollis sensed that Wes would just as soon ride off, so he backed down. "All right, Carson. I'll draw up a paper for you. But I'm just holding the land by customary use, except for this section the house is on. All I'll be doin' is givin' away my own claim to the meadows. You may still have to fight the Grubers to hold it.''

"That'll do," Wes said, satisfied. "I'll start buildin' up there to set my mark."

"Don't forget what I hired you for."

"What about the Taylors?"

The rancher shrugged. "That old man's tough as nails, and so's his granddaughter, but her mother's a lady. I got no fight with them. They moved in on Gruber grass, south of the river, and Gruber's tryin' to run 'em off."

"I reckon I'll go talk to 'em. They might know somethin'."

"You do that, but don't take chances. Grubers will be all over that range. And from what I've seen of 'em, they ain't lettin' Sal's killing be set aside. They'll be huntin' you, sure as shootin'."

Wes and the rancher hesitated, then reluctantly shook hands to seal the agreement. Hollis went into the house, and Wes and Haney waited until he came out with the handwritten deed, delivering it to Wes, who shoved it inside his shirt. The two men glared at each other, then Hollis went back inside.

Wes stood staring at the door. Where was Angela?

Reluctant and yet relieved that seeing her had been

postponed to give him time to prepare, Wes followed Haney to the corrals, where they unsaddled.

Haney grunted. "If you wanted to hurt him, you sure did. Turkey Creek's where he'd planned to build a house for his wife afore she died."

Wes was uneasy with Haney's words, so he switched his thoughts and turned to the foreman. "Since the Taylors are in the middle, they might have some information I can use. Want to come along?"

"Can't tomorrow, but someday I wouldn't mind. I saw that Mrs. Taylor once in town. Helped her load up her wagon. Fine-lookin' woman and a widow. Except I got nothin' to offer. Forty years in the saddle and that's all I got, besides my horse. She wouldn't want an old broken-up cowhand."

"Don't try to read a woman's mind," Wes said. "It can't be done. And there's nothin' they like better than takin' in strays. Now, how do I get there?"

"Straight south, but be careful. First off, that Silas Gruber's mean as sin and he ain't gonna forget you killed his son. Don't matter how fast you are if you're back shot."

"Where was Randy Hollis murdered?"

"It was right near the old hangin' tree. Rope's still there, hangin' from a cottonwood, right near the ford. You can't miss it. Head straight south toward the red-rock ridge. Randy was found shot dead center and half in the water.'' Haney's voice failed him, and he turned away.

Wes didn't sleep that night. He had carried a grudge against Hollis so long it had become a pain in his gut, and now he had shaken the man's hand. It went against his grain, but he had wanted the bargain sealed. Maybe he would never build in Turkey Creek, especially now that he knew the reason Hollis wanted it.

While Wes was tossing and turning, Reed Hollis was sitting in his leather chair and looking up as Angela came down the stairs. He loved his daughter. She reminded him of his late wife, having the same pretty face and dimpled cheeks. Angela's dark-brown hair was worn in large curls down the nape of her neck. Her blue eyes were still dazed with sleep. She was wearing a gingham dress with lace at the throat.

"Father, I didn't mean to sleep so long."

"Are you feelin' better?"

She nodded as she took a seat near him.

"You know, honey," he said, "you ain't been awful happy since you got betrothed to that Cliff Sellers."

"No, it's not that. It's just that I haven't been the same since we lost Randy. And I know you haven't slept, either. I hear you pacing the floor. But where's Reggie?"

"Out ridin', I think. But right now, we got a visitor."

She brightened. "Wes Carson?"

"Down at the bunkhouse."

"Why didn't you wake me?"

"Honey, nothin's changed. He's still a gunfighter. And he come, like you asked. Quit his job on account of you."

She smiled, pleased. "So he still loves me."

"All I know is, I made a deal with him. He'll help us, as long as I give 'im Turkey Creek Meadows."

"Father, you didn't."

"We can't hold it nohow. Lost a good man up there. And there's been a lot of trailin' through there, so I figure rustlers are usin' that route. I don't want to lose any more men, not over a few strays. And that's where the sheriff found that old prospector's body. It just ain't worth it."

She frowned, arms folded. "So he really hasn't changed. He only thinks of himself and how much he can get paid. I'll never know how he could say he loved me but not quit his job with the Army. He was so selfish. I've never forgiven him for that."

"Well, he did come when he got your letter. And he's already faced down Sal Gruber and killed him."

She listened in awe as he told her the story.

\* \* \*

Meanwhile, the Gruber front room was hot with argument. In front of the blazing stone hearth, Seth was facing his mother. They had already buried Sal, and she was fresh out of tears.

Martha Gruber, prim in appearance with clear blue eyes, a small nose and gray-blond hair, had more power than appeared in her small size.

"It ain't right," she said sharply.

"Ma," Seth argued, "there was a big crowd, and Pa don't want no town trouble. I couldn't do nothin' with everyone watchin', but you don't worry none. We'll get Carson, one way or another."

She sat down with arms folded. "That Carson killed my Sal. Folks will be laughin' at us. You get rid of Carson now."

"It won't be easy."

"You got a lot of hired guns out there. Set 'em on Carson before he gets too big for his britches. I don't care how it gets done."

"I ain't sure anyone can beat 'im." When his mother stiffened in anger, he shrugged. "Well, maybe Brazos can take 'im. Or Maddox. And you know, Ma, Simon and Sloan been practicin' every day."

"I don't want to lose any more sons," she snapped. "You do as I say."

"What about Turkey Creek?"

"Stay away from there until your Pa gets back from Butte with your brothers. Right now, you just get rid of Wes Carson."

"Soon's Brazos gets back from the Taylors' place tomorrow, I'll talk to 'im," Sal said. "But you know Pa wants us to do our own fightin'."

"Your Pa's a man, that's why. But he ain't here, and I am, so just do what I say."

With that, Martha picked up her knitting, her hands cold as she thought of her lost son, her insides hot as she longed for revenge.

Unaware of the threat, Wes slept restlessly, then awakened before dawn. He ate at the cookshed with some of the men, all experienced hands with stories to tell. Pete and Barney introduced him all around.

He left them to their coffee and went out to saddle his stallion. The sky was crimson in the east as first light began to break.

He mounted, then paused as he saw a young cowpuncher walking downhill from the main house. He had the look of Reed Hollis, but he was in his early twenties, and his eyes were small and black. He wore two guns and smelled of whiskey. His hat was pushed back as he gazed up at Wes.

"So you're Wes Carson. I'm Reggie Hollis."

Wes leaned on the pommel. "Glad to meet you."

"I reckon you think you can take on the whole Gruber bunch by yourself."

"Wasn't plannin' to. Figured you'd help."

Reggie hesitated, not sure if Wes was funnin' him.

Then he grunted and went into the cookshed to talk to the men.

Wes glanced toward the house, wondering when he would see Angela, yet afraid to see her, uncertain if he could handle it. He rode on south over the rolling hills and through more of the Hollis cattle.

The clouds on the northern horizon were yet to move south and shield the brightness of the sun. There were scattered aspens and pines, groves of cottonwoods along the creeks, and rich green grass with blue and yellow wildflowers.

It was after noon when he reached the river. He found a ford where the water was shallow. Yet he knew that a storm could turn that shimmering river into a flood. And there in the grove of cottonwoods part of a rope still dangled a foot down from a high limb. There were no remaining signs.

Wes rode on south over the hills at a lope, his hand on his holster, the sunshine and wind in his face. When he reined up in a grove of aspens, he could see down into the flats. A ranch house and outbuildings were set on the roll of a hill to his right, with a large barn farther out. Some thirty red chickens were in a wire pen with a chicken house behind them, and nearby was a corn patch.

Three men on horseback were in front of the house. Standing on the small porch was an older man with a crutch under his right arm. His white hair was gleaming in the sunlight as he balanced a rifle with his left arm. He was wearing britches over his red underwear, but no shirt.

One of the riders was a man of average height, silver conchos on his hatband, a leather vest over his white shirt. One of his companions wore fancy twin guns and a pinched top hat. The third was wearing a buckskin coat with fringe.

Instinctively, Wes started riding downhill toward the meadow and the ranch house. The man with the fancy hatband appeared to be the leader and was talking to the rancher.

Two mares in the corral, sighting Wes's stallion, began to pace and nicker, kicking up their heels. One of the riders turned in the saddle. Suddenly, all movement stopped as they watched Wes riding across the flat.

As Wes began to ride up higher ground toward the house, all three riders reined about to face him. The leader sat stiff in the saddle, his big, almost buglike brown eyes adding to his evil appearance. His face was square, his nose hooked. "What you want here, mister?" he demanded.

"I came to visit with Mr. Taylor."

"Well, you ain't welcome, so move on. This is Gruber land, and there ain't no more room."

The rancher, his rifle wavering in his grasp, looked up at Wes curiously. "Do I know you?"

"Wes Carson."

Instantly, the leader of the intruders began to

sneer. "So you're the saddle tramp who killed Sal Gruber."

"It was a fair fight," the rancher said. "My granddaughter saw it."

The gunman straightened. "My name's Chuck Maddox. I figure you've heard of me, so you'd better ride out of here, Carson."

Wes casually glanced at the other two men. One was a likeness of Maddox, without the buglike eyes, and younger. The third man was maybe sixty, his buckskin coat open to show an Indian amulet.

Wes had heard of Maddox, who had left a trail of dead men on his way to Montana a few years ago. He watched the killer turn his horse about to look directly at him.

"Carson, we can have it out now, or you can head out."

"Chuck," the man in buckskin said, "you'd better clear this with Gruber."

Maddox shrugged and leaned back. "Maybe so. He probably wants you himself, Carson. So get ready to meet your maker."

The old rancher snarled. "Get off my land, Maddox."

With a laugh, Maddox swung his horse about and headed downhill, the others following. Wes leaned on the pommel, watching them go.

Abruptly, the younger gunman reined about and came within five feet of Wes. His mouth twisted into a challenging sneer. "Carson, I'm the Brazos Kid. Maybe you heard of me, from over in Kansas," he said.

"Nope."

Brazos straightened. "Maybe ol' man Gruber would appreciate my getting rid of you, but I don't fancy it from the saddle. If you'll step down, we'll just see who rides away from here."

Aware that the other two riders had reined up some fifty feet away, Wes dug in his heels and spurred his stallion forward as Brazos started to step down. The horse's shoulder struck Brazos on the left arm and hip, startling his horse so that it spun.

Brazos fell haphazardly, his boot caught in the stirrup for just a second. Then he landed on his left shoulder and rump, loudly hitting the ground. His horse ran off and circled, tossing its head. Brazos was stunned. As he started to rise, Wes dismounted and was upon him, grabbing him from behind, his right arm around the youth's neck, choking him.

Brazos gasped for air, kicking and fighting, trying to get free, but Wes held on tight. As Brazos gradually slumped, Wes let him go. The youth fell to his knees, grabbing his throat and coughing.

Wes backed away and mounted his horse, aware the others had ridden back.

The man in buckskin dismounted and led Brazos's horse over to him. He took the youth's arm, but he jerked free and got to his feet on his own, snarling in a hoarse voice, "Get away, Grange. I'm all right."

Wes straightened. "Rio Grange?"

The man mounted and nodded. "That's right."

"From Austin, Texas?"

Again the man nodded. Brazos managed to swing into the saddle and glare at both Rio and Wes, but he had no color.

Wes ignored Brazos and concentrated on Rio. "I've heard of you. You were at the battle of Adobe Walls. And you scouted for Colonel MacKenzie."

"Them days are gone," Rio said.

"One of MacKenzie's scouts was on a trail drive with me. Named Cohen. Told me how the Comanche would circle your columns by moonlight, hit hard, then disappear. You and Cohen were together until Quanah Parker surrendered."

Rio's face darkened. "I heard some about you and the Army. They said if anyone could track an Apache, it was you. We meet in town, I'll buy you a drink."

"Forget it, Rio," Chuck Maddox said, his face flushed with anger. "You work for Gruber now, and you answer to me."

Brazos fought to speak, his voice a whisper. "We'll meet again, Carson. Maybe next time you'll face up like a man."

The three gunmen turned and rode away across the meadow, Brazos still clutching his throat. When they were out of sight, Wes turned to look down at the elderly rancher in front of the house and grinned as he said, "Mighty unfriendly around here."

"What do you want, Carson?"

"Just figured you needed help."

"Not from the likes of you."

"I see where your granddaughter gets her manners."

The old man grimaced, glaring up at him. Then his blue eyes began to twinkle and his white mustache twitched. Now he was chuckling.

"All right, Carson. Step down."

Wes dismounted and loosened the cinch, then left his stallion at the hitching post. He followed the limping old man inside the rather small house. The front room had a fireplace but only a few pieces of furniture. On the walls were several fine paintings of Sioux and of trail herds. Wes paused to admire them.

Taylor sat down on a leather chair, dropping his crutch. He followed Wes's gaze to the striking pictures. "My granddaughter paints."

"A woman painter?"

"She don't do nothin' like other women."

Wes continued to admire the oils. "Them Sioux could ride clear out of that frame."

"We seen enough of 'em at Laramie and comin' up the Bozeman. You see, she ain't been much for tradition, and she can do just about anything she sets her mind to. But I been worried she ain't never gonna settle down.''

A woman came out of the back bedroom. She was comely, maybe in her late forties, a little plump but with a nice face and clear green eyes. She was wearing a robe, her dark auburn hair sprinkled with gray and wrapped in a bun behind her neck.

''You must have been talking about Cindy,'' she said with a smile. ''She's a worry, that one.''

''This here's my daughter-in-law, Clarisa, Cindy's ma. She ain't been well ever since my boy died back in Missouri.''

''After what I saw through the window,'' the woman said, ''I'm feeling a whole lot better.''

Wes removed his hat. ''Well, ma'am, Mr. Haney was right.''

''Mr. Haney?'' she asked with interest. ''You mean the foreman on the Little River H?''

''Yes, ma'am. He said you were a right handsome woman.''

Shyly, she fussed with her hair and went over to the iron stove in the corner. She served them coffee, then went back to her room. Taylor frowned, watching her close the door behind her.

''It's been three years since my boy died.''

''She sure lit up when I mentioned Haney.''

''I like the man all right. He's got integrity and he's got honor, and you don't see much of that since the War Between the States.''

"Well, he's sure interested in her."

Wes sat on a wooden rocking chair. He enjoyed moving it back and forth, putting his head back. It was finely hewn and almost silent.

"My granddaughter made that. She took an old chair and fixed it up, then put runners on it."

Wes frowned. "Is there anything she can't do?"

"Yeah, she can't do anything I tell her."

They both grinned, and Taylor sipped his coffee, studying Wes carefully before speaking. He seemed to be trying to decide if Wes was trustworthy.

"Cindy says you took Sal Gruber easy."

"May have looked that way."

"The Grubers are goin' to be plenty mad about it. Silas Gruber will want you dead. The fastest are Simon and Sloan, the older boys, and they're the most dangerous because they keep their heads. Then there's Seth, the youngest, kind of clumsy. All of 'em would like nothin' better than to marry Cindy."

"She want that?"

"The only way to get Cindy to do something is to tell her you'll whup her if she doesn't."

"You ever do that?"

"Whup her? Nah. Never could catch her. She runs like a pronghorn. Swims like an eel. Rides like a Comanche."

"But would you want her to hitch up with a Gruber?"

"Stoke up that fire, will you?"

"If you answer my question."

Taylor shrugged. "I don't want her to marry up with any of 'em. But I can't tell her what to do, like I said."

"Where is she now?"

"Countin' cattle. She and that mongrel she brung home. Little rascal barked at me. Anyhow, our last two hands quit and took off. Figure they got scared. Makes four we lost."

Wes knelt and stoked up the fire in the hearth. The flames crackled and spat. He shoved in more wood. Then he returned to the rocker, impressed even more with Cindy's handiwork. The woman had more than an ordinary level of intelligence, and she was gifted.

"But you listen to me, Wes. Why are you stickin' around? You workin' for Hollis?"

"I made a deal to get my own spread. Seems Hollis is plenty worried about the Grubers. Wants me to scare 'em. And I guess you're in the middle."

"Yeah, I know. We coulda trailed our herd out and left here a long time ago. But I ain't givin' up this land. They'll have to kill me first."

"What about Cindy?"

"She agrees."

"But she's a woman. She could get hurt."

Taylor frowned. "I know. Listen, you're stayin' for supper. Soon's she gets back. Seems like she shoulda been back a long time ago. But I got throwed and can't sit a saddle, and I'm gettin' worried.''

''I was headed for town, but I'll go look for her.''

''Thanks. You head due west. The herd's spread up along the river about now. We had a good crop of calves, but the wolves been comin' down out of the mountains. The ranchers are all payin' a bounty. I'm worried about her.''

Wes stood up, setting his cup back on the table near the stove. ''How'd she get that scar on her chin?''

''She got bucked off when she was a youngster, cut her chin, but she got right back on again. Say, I've been admirin' your spurs. Mighty fancy. Mexican?''

''I reckon. Got 'em from a friend down in Texas. Wear 'em for luck. I just like the jingle, I guess.''

''Bet you didn't wear 'em while you was scoutin'.''

''No, and a few times I even pulled off my boots.''

They grinned at each other as they both pictured Wes barefoot in the sand, sneaking up on Apaches, except that Wes could still feel the sand between his toes.

Outside in the afternoon sun, Wes tightened the cinch and mounted, riding his prancing stallion past the mares in the corral and heading over the hillside and down to the next meadow.

Clouds moving in from the north gradually caught

up with the sun. Now the land was shadowed in green and gray, spotted with the sprinkle of yellow flowers.

It was late afternoon when he saw the herd, some two hundred head. There were maybe fifty head of beef, an old scraggly longhorn bull with scars on the shoulder and rump, and one mean-looking cross-breed bull, its nose curled up, evidently the he-bull of this outfit. The rest were cows with white-faced or brockle-faced calves.

The herd was grazing near the southern banks of the Little River, some under the cottonwoods and aspens. There was no sign of a horse or of Cindy. Wes rode through the herd, and one cow charged as he scurried past.

On the next rise, he looked in all directions but saw nothing except a few more head of cattle. He rode along the riverbank, away from the herd. Then several miles farther, he saw buzzards circling. Black ugly devils sailing the wind and zeroing in on something.

Worried, he urged his stallion into a lope. Soon, in a grove of cottonwoods, he reined up. There was the carcass of a young calf, torn to shreds. Farther away in the trees, the defending cow had been gutted alive and had bled to death.

It seemed to have happened not many hours before.

There were large wolf tracks in the mud, crossed

by the hoofprints of a shod horse and trailed by the small prints of a mongrel dog. There in the deep grass was a dead gray wolf, shot through the head. Bellies full, the wolves must have decided not to take on Cindy's rifle, and they could outrun the yapping dog. So far, she was lucky.

Wes grimly followed the tracks as best he could through the grass and then headed south toward the blue range of mountains. There were five wolves left in the pack. And Cindy's horse was right on their tracks.

Toward evening, he saw the body of another dead wolf, shot clean through the head. It must have turned on her. It was a huge gray animal, nearly a hundred pounds, yellow eyes staring into space, long legs stretched out.

Wes swallowed hard. One mistake, and the wolves could pull her horse down. He knew she couldn't let them go, because they would be back for more of the herd. The wolves knew where their next easy meal would be. But she was taking a terrible chance.

Wes urged his stallion forward. As he trailed Cindy's horse and the four wolves ever southward in the twilight, he was grim and worried. He knew about wolves. They would come in packs, separate cattle from the herd, and tear up calves.

He crossed a small creek where a canyon cut through the land. As he neared the foothills where scattered pines darkened the slopes, he saw a rise of boulders. And at the foot of a steep trail that led to some aspens, a horse lay dead and gutted, still strapped to a saddle.

Frantic, Wes rode past the animal and up the steep trail. He saw signs where the wolves had turned on their pursuer. Near her slip-and-slide boot prints, a rifle had slid down into a crack in the rocks where it had fallen out of reach. He could see where she had run up the trail, sliding several times.

There in the brush was the little dog, bloody but maybe still alive. Signs told him that the dog had distracted the wolves long enough to give her a chance.

Wes regretfully had to ride past the wounded dog and hurry on, and now he saw the wolves, resting and snarling at each other, all four gathered at the foot of an aspen. A woman's boot, torn and covered with blood, lay near one of the largest wolves.

His stallion snorted and reared. Wes drew his Winchester from the scabbard. The wolves turned on him, lips curled back, snarling, their fangs bared.

He fired, hitting one between the eyes. It dropped. The others scattered. He fired again, dropping one, then another. The last wolf sprang up the slope, scurrying for cover, but Wes fired again. It dropped, rose and kept running. He shot once more, and the animal spun, then rolled over.

He rode forward, ignoring the dead animals even

as his stallion pranced nervously, tossing its head. He looked from the torn boot up the trunk of the tall aspen.

Clinging to the narrow branches was a woman. Her bloody left foot was dangling. He saw her skirts and left arm. He rode forward and looked up from the other side. She was ashen, her red hair falling about her face. Her hands were bleeding from her climb. She stared down at him with sudden tears in her eyes. But she couldn't move.

"It's all right now," he called.

Then he dismounted, fearing she was going to faint and just let go.

He was right. She came tumbling off the tree. He jumped and reached for her as she fell through the branches. He caught her before she hit the ground, sweeping her up in his arms.

She seemed lifeless, like a child in his arms. Her lips were parted. There were scratches on her face, and her jacket was torn in several places. He recovered her boot, set her on the saddle against the pommel, and went for the little dog. He picked up the bleeding animal, its eyes fixed on him as it tried to snarl.

"You don't give up, do you?" Wes grunted with a grin.

With more respect for the little dog, Wes held it up for Cindy's waiting arms and she embraced it.

He stepped up behind them, holding her limp against his chest.

They had to get away from the dead wolves. The carcasses could attract other predators. The sky was dark with clouds. Night fell suddenly, dense and black around them.

Wes rode through the trees and down the slope, past the dead horse and across the hills. Cindy leaned against him, cold and shivering as she kept the little dog in her arms. It was already sprinkling. He was glad he had brought along his bedroll and possibles.

He had to find shelter and cleanse her wounds. He remembered the creek and small canyon. There would be some protection under the overhanging boulders.

It was raining when he reached the creek and rode into the narrow canyon. He dismounted under the shelter of the rocks and let her slide into his arms. He laid her down on the grass, the dog rolling aside but still trying to snarl.

Wes brought forth his bedroll, spreading one blanket, and reached down to lift Cindy. She opened her eyes and gazed at him as he moved her onto the blanket and drew another across her. Then he soaked his bandanna in the creek and brought it back to wash her face and hands. She just lay silent, breathing hard, her eyes following his every movement.

He washed her foot several times, then used the brandy he carried for such purposes to wash the wound again. She winced in pain, and he wrapped her foot in a spare bandanna.

After he had carried the little dog down to the creek and bathed its wounds, he built a fire from brambles and fallen branches. The bright, colorful flames shot upward, while the rain fell heavily from the edges of the rocks.

Cindy cuddled the nearly lifeless dog. "We can't stay here," she whispered.

"I know. There could be a flood. But I had to give you a chance. Didn't want you to get blood poisonin'."

"You saved my life. Why?"

He didn't answer but gazed at her lovely face, at the glistening shine of her eyes, the freckles on her nose, the way her flaming hair looked silken. This woman could paint Sioux Indians, build rocking chairs, and hunt wolves. She wasn't quite real.

Angela had been more believable, so gentle and always with a smile, her dark eyes dancing whenever he was near. He had managed a kiss one night near the wagons inside the fort. He still remembered her soft touch on his face.

Trying to control his thoughts, he went back to rub down his stallion. They would have to leave soon. The rain could come flooding down the canyon unexpectedly.

As he saddled his buckskin, Cindy sat up and said, "I was foolish, wasn't I?"

"Maybe."

"I just thought I could catch them before they got to the mountains. I never thought they would turn on me. I mean, they ran when I came and shot the first one."

"You ever hunt wolves before?"

"No."

"You and your grandfather have to get help. You can't do this alone."

"Before he was thrown from his horse, he was as hardy as any man. We would have done all right. But the doctor said he cracked some ribs and damaged his knee. We'll find hands."

"And if you don't?"

"Then Gruber will run right over us. He keeps saying we're on his land, you know."

"I hear the Grubers are sweet on you."

She flushed, drawing the blanket tighter around her. "Women are scarce out here, Mr. Carson."

"Can you ride?"

"Yes, thank you."

He reached down to offer his hand, taking hers and pulling her to her feet. She stood close, her weight on her good foot, as she glanced at the little dog on the grass. Nervous and uncomfortable, Wes wanted to pull away.

She smiled up at him. "For an ugly man, you sure looked beautiful back there at the bottom of that tree."

"For an ugly woman, you didn't look so bad yourself."

They gazed at each other a long moment, her hand still small and cold in his big one. Rain was falling heavily in the creek and running off the rocks near them, noisy and insistent. He felt as if he were in a trance.

At length, he released her hand and turned to the stallion. He donned his leather coat and pulled his slicker about her.

"Can you step up alone?"

"My foot is too sore."

He turned and put his hands at her waist, then hesitated. She was so close, so feminine, so vulnerable.

As he started to lift her, she slid her hand around his neck and pulled his head down. Her lips rested like velvet on his. He caught his breath, taken by surprise, his heart so wild he thought it would leap from his chest. He didn't close his eyes, but gazed down at her long lashes resting on her cheeks.

Slowly, she drew back. "Thank you, Wes. I couldn't have held on much longer."

Breath tight in his lungs, he lifted her up onto the saddle against the pommel. Then he handed her the dog, which was breathing more regularly now. He swung up behind her, and she slid against him as he adjusted the slicker about her.

"We'll have to get you to the doctor," he mumbled.

"No need. He's coming out to see my grandfather tomorrow."

He turned the stallion into the rain and they headed out of the canyon, over the hills. He felt that she slept most of the way. She had lost a lot of blood and was exhausted, but Wes was more worried about her foot, because of possible blood poisoning or tetanus.

## Chapter Three

Riding back with Cindy in his embrace, Wes felt his arm about her become stiff from the wet and cold. Rain poured off his hat. The slicker was pulled over her head, and he was some shelter. The stallion picked its way through the mud and grass.

When they reached the ranch house, it was long after midnight. A lamp was burning inside, light visible through the cracks in the window shutters. The rain was still heavy as Wes shook Cindy awake, finding her face and hands hot with fever, but the dog seemed to be recovering.

"You're home," he said.

He stepped down, then reached for her. Holding the little dog, she slid into his arms, and he carried her, water pouring off his hat and her slicker.

She lay in his arms without movement, her head

47

against his chest. He kicked at the door several times. The window shutter slid aside and Taylor peered out. Then the rancher hurriedly let them inside, barring the door behind them. A warm fire was blazing in the hearth.

The rancher was frantic as Wes set Cindy down in the leather chair near the fireplace. Clarisa came out in her robe, her face colorless, and she knelt at her daughter's side, caressing her arm and hair. Cindy lay back, smiling at them as her grandfather covered her and her dog with a blanket.

"Wes saved us from the wolves," she said, and recounted the tale.

Wes nodded toward the little dog. "That critter was the bravest, and you can bet on it. He's not even half the size of a wolf."

"I won't be funnin' him no more," Taylor said, "but, Cindy, you shouldn't have followed them wolves."

"They would have come back," she said. "We couldn't camp out there every night."

Wes poured them cups of hot coffee, and Cindy drank hers, shivering with cold though her skin was burning.

As her mother fussed over her, Wes knelt and pulled the bandanna from her foot. The wound looked all right, yet it had to be the cause of her fever. He could see the teeth marks deep in her flesh, and he was worried.

"Up on the shelf, there's some slippery elm bark fixed up for poultice," Taylor told him. "And some towels."

Wes wet the towel and wrapped the remedy inside, then pressed it directly on the wound, using the towel to wrap it around her foot and cool her flesh. He went for another towel, wet it from the pitcher, and laid it across her face.

As Wes and her mother tried to cool Cindy and lower her fever, Taylor told her about the three gunmen and how Wes had manhandled the Brazos Kid. Though still burning with fever, Cindy was obviously impressed.

When Clarisa asked Wes to help her get Cindy to her bed, Cindy protested, but Wes carefully lifted her and carried her into the small bedroom. The dog followed close behind.

Once Cindy was settled on her bed Wes pulled off her boot carefully and felt how cold her right foot was. He peeled the towel from her left foot and found her skin to be white as snow. He looked up, her foot still in his hand as he wrapped it with the poultice once more. "You've got to help us, Cindy. You've got to tell us what feels different."

She nodded, and he left her in her mother's care, closing the door on them as he rejoined Taylor in the other room.

"Don't fret, son," Taylor said. "She's been through worse. Once a rattler got her. Another time, she near drowned in the river. Horse fell on her once. Steer got her with his horn, right on the rump. But she pulled through.''

"I'm worried about tetanus. We got to sweat her out.''

"It's rainin'. How we gonna do that?''

"Buckets with hot rocks and water. We can do it right there in her room. Might as well sweat the dog too.''

"There are two buckets in here and more in the barn.''

"I'll get 'em.''

The two men set about methodically heating and steaming Cindy's room. Rocks were placed in the fire, then scooped into buckets of water and carried inside, over and over.

Soon Cindy was lying in a room full of steam, sweat pouring from her. Scotty, the little dog, was on the floor, tongue hanging. Cindy's mother brought her hot soup and then lime water to drink. They kept her covered with blankets.

After a time, the dog staggered back into the other room, shaking his head and lapping up water offered by Taylor. But Cindy remained in her bed.

Soon, delirium took over. Cindy was frantically kicking and squealing, as if the wolf was still grabbing her left foot and trying to pull her back down the tree. Her mother hugged her. This calmed her, but it was hours before the steam sweated the fury from her body.

Once she whined angrily, "Jimmy, you stop that!"

Her mother looked distressed. "He was a little boy in the first grade, used to try to kiss her. She would get so mad at him, but she had a crush on him at the same time."

When at last Cindy slept peacefully, the fever gone, Wes drew aside the blanket to look at her foot. The skin was still white except for the initial bruises. There was no blood poisoning, at least not so far.

They removed the buckets and left her door open for fresh air to enter. Scotty trotted back inside to lie down by her bed, and her mother curled up in a chair near her.

Exhausted, Taylor hobbled to his leather chair and sat down clumsily. It was obvious he was hurting badly. "How did you learn all that?" he asked.

"Indians do it, I reckon, but I learned it from a trail boss. We had a man who was mauled by a bear. We saved him by steamin' him in a tent, like the Indians do. I also saw him fix the man's leg when the blood poisoning came. Saw him cut the vein and let the blood come out. I'm glad we didn't have to do that."

Taylor lay back in his chair. "Thank you, Wes."

"Cindy said the doctor was coming."

"Be here in the mornin'. Can you wait?"

Wes nodded and slumped in the rocker, weary and half asleep. Rain was heavy on the roof, wind slamming against the walls and windows. Before he knew it, both he and the rancher were deep in slumber. When Wes awakened before dawn, the rancher was on a cot. Wes checked on Cindy, then spread a blanket by the fire and went back to sleep.

When he awakened again, it was late morning. The smell of coffee and bacon was exhilarating.

Taylor was hobbling about with his crutch, nearly falling every few minutes. Yet he had prepared a great breakfast. Wes tore his gaze from the sizzling bacon and went into Cindy's room. Her mother was asleep in the chair, a blanket drawn over her. Scotty was at the foot of the bed, snoring softly.

Wes opened the window to let in fresh air, then knelt by Cindy's bed. She was sleeping peacefully. He spread her damp hair away from her lovely face. She had so much talent and courage, he was grateful she was alive.

He stood up, bent over, and kissed her forehead gently.

Then he straightened and turned to see Taylor watching him from the doorway. Wes shrugged away the kiss and went to the door, waiting for the old man to move. Taylor was studying him intently, but at length the rancher turned around and went back to the table.

Taylor sat down and allowed Wes to serve the bacon, beans, and hot coffee.

"She'll be hungry when she wakes up," Wes said.

"When I think of her out there with them wolves, I get scared all over again. Can you imagine climbing a tree while one of 'em's hanging on to your boot, pullin' it off, then grabbin' for the rest of you?"

"They were high-country wolves. They had no fear of man when they came down."

"You're probably right. I'm sure glad she's alive. And I reckon I have you to thank for that, Wes, but what I just saw in there makes me mighty curious. What are your intentions?"

"None, Mr. Taylor. I just have a lot of admiration for your granddaughter."

"Well, I was thinkin' she needs a man like you. This country ain't easy on women, you know. Got to have a tough hombre lookin' after 'em."

"I ain't one for settlin' down."

"Ain't right for women to be alone, even a wild one like Cindy. If I could find a man for Clarisa, maybe she'd get well, but she ain't got over losin' my son back in Missouri. Horse fell on him."

"Sorry to hear that."

"Anyhow, I thought I was bringin' 'em to a peaceful place to start over. Now the Grubers have been tryin' to run us off. They could have killed Randy Hollis and done the rustlin'. And I figure if it ain't them, then someone's tryin' to send a message to Reed Hollis.''

''Like what?''

''Like stay on his side of the river and not branch out, and stay away from Turkey Creek, what runs south into Little River a piece west of here. You ride north into the prettiest canyon you ever saw. Grass so tall and sweet, you just want to roll in it. Both ranchers want it, but Hollis had first claim.''

Wes couldn't help but smile at the thought of owning that land, but even if he had taken it from Hollis, he might not be able to hold it against the Grubers.

They could hear the horses nickering. Wes shoved the wooden windowpane aside and looked out at the gray sky and soaked earth. It had stopped raining, and coming up the trail was a buggy with a white horse.

''Must be the doctor,'' Wes said. ''I'll go meet 'im.''

''There's some hay and grain in the shed by the corrals. Feed the horses, will you?''

Wes nodded and went outside. He waited as the doctor reined up and swung down with his bag. The squat little man peered at Wes over his spectacles.

''There's a sick girl in there,'' Wes said.

The doctor, surprised, turned and hurried inside. Wes led the buggy horse over to the corrals so he could feed and water it, along with the other horses.

His stallion, in a pen by itself, reared and snorted and kicked.

Wes stroked its neck as he thought of Taylor's words about Cindy. Five years ago, Angela had thought Wes was too rough and wild, living too violent a life. Her father had seen him as a gunman and refused permission. Now another rancher was telling him he was the right kind of man.

It was five years too late, and that hurt plenty.

When Wes returned to the house, the doctor had already seen Cindy and was sharing coffee at the table with Taylor and Clarisa, who was smiling brightly. In fact, Clarisa's hair was combed out and she was wearing a dress, which seemed to make Taylor very happy.

"Wes," the rancher said, "Doc here says you saved Cindy's life."

The doctor nodded. "She would have gone into convulsions. But I hear tell you had a run-in with Maddox and Brazos. You oughta ride out, son."

"He's too stubborn."

The voice was Cindy's. They turned to see her in the doorway, leaning on the doorjamb with her bandaged left foot off the floor. She was wearing a robe over her nightgown and a slipper on her right foot. Scotty was at her side, looking well and frisky.

Taylor stumbled clumsily to his feet, gripping the table. "You should be in bed. Doc said to keep your foot up."

"I can do that in your chair," she said, smiling.

Wes, feeling awkward, got to his feet and went to help her. He slid his right arm around her, and she looked up at him with a smile. Scotty growled and snarled, but he didn't attack. He barked twice at Wes, two little yips. The others laughed.

Wes didn't mind half carrying her to the leather chair. He helped her sit and elevated her foot on a stool. Then he covered her with a blanket. The firelight was glistening in her eyes.

"That dog," the doctor said, "come into town half dead with a bullet hole in 'im a couple of months ago. So I cleaned him up and nursed him awhile, and then the town sort of adopted him. When Wes got to helpin' Cindy, that was the first time that dog even showed any interest in anything. But it sure took to ranch livin'."

Cindy smiled. "He likes to chew on Wes."

Wes sat back at the table and sipped his coffee as he glared at the little dog, which glared back at him. "I'll be heading back to town," he said.

The doctor took Taylor and Clarisa into the back room to examine them both. Cindy was gazing at Wes with a smile so sweet it would have curled the tail of a grizzly.

"Doc says you saved my life a second time."

Abruptly, the cup of coffee slipped in her hand, spilling hot liquid on her blanket and robe. She jumped and squealed. Wes grabbed a towel and came to kneel and rub quickly. Suddenly embarrassed at what he was doing, he handed her the towel. He got back to his feet and sat down at the table, studying her.

''Who was Jimmy?''

''Jimmy?''

''You were goin' on about him when you were out of your head in there.''

''Oh, Jimmy. He grew up to be a real idiot.'' She smiled, then gazed at him curiously. ''Are you married, Wes?''

''No.'' His face was burning as he stood up. ''I'll be on my way.''

''Not until you put me back in bed.''

Uneasy, he bent down and put his hands behind her waist and under her knees, lifting her easily, the blanket still over her. He looked around for the dog, but it had fallen asleep by the hearth. Cindy slid her arms up his chest, one hand at his neck.

''Am I heavy?''

''Sure are.''

He carried her, and she felt small. He kicked the door open and walked inside. The room was still damp, even though the window had been opened.

Before he could set her down, she squirmed and clung to him. ''I've changed my mind. It's too cold in here.''

Irritated, he turned and walked back to the front room as she rested her head on his chest. He was about to bend down to set her in the chair when her grandfather hobbled back in with the doctor, Clarisa at their heels. They paused and stared as Wes lowered Cindy.

"My room was too cold," she said cheerfully.

"Tomorrow's Sunday," Clarisa said, fussing with her hair. "I would like it very much, Wes, if you and Mr. Haney were to come for Sunday supper, around sunset."

Taylor looked surprised but mighty pleased, but Cindy's smile was uneasy. "Well, you did say I'd be inviting you for supper, Wes. I guess you earned it. Will you come?"

As skittish as Wes was feeling, he couldn't say no, or Haney would be disappointed. "Sure, we'd like that a lot."

After more coffee, Wes left the Taylors and headed his stallion eastward toward Shotgun Wells, knowing all the while that the Grubers would be lying in wait for him.

Or he could be back shot, without ceremony.

And when he entered the saloon that evening, a dozen men who were strangers to him were scattered about, watching him as if he was already a dead man. And there at the end of the bar was Reggie Hollis, drinking one glass of whiskey after another. When he saw Wes, he straightened, then turned away.

Wes took a corner table, his back to the wall, and

ordered a meal and coffee. He ate slowly while keeping an eye on Reggie and the other men.

It was then that Rio Grange entered. When he saw Wes, he walked over and sat with him, ordering coffee and keeping his back to the wall as well. The man's weathered face was lined with age and experience, skin crinkling around his pale eyes. He spoke quietly.

"I came lookin' for you. Ma Gruber's put a price on your head."

"That so?"

"Well, not so's you could arrest her for it. She just said if someone was to tell her they'd shot you down for good, she'd pay a hundred dollars. She's madder'n a wet hen."

"You know anything about Randy Hollis?"

Rio shrugged. "I know he was killed."

"Got any ideas who done it?"

"No. I hear Randy was askin' the sheriff to do somethin' about the rustlin' and was threatenin' to get the U.S. Marshal here. Maybe the Grubers had a price on Randy's head. You'd better be thinkin' about how bad you wanta stay around here."

Wes sipped his coffee slowly. "My deal with Hollis will help me get my own spread." *And,* he thought, *recover a bit of justice.*

"That your only reason? Because if it is, dead men don't get much chance to herd cows."

"You know anything about Turkey Creek Meadows?"

"Heard about it. Gruber wants it real bad."

"He say why?"

"Nope, but there's somethin' there he wants."

Wes looked up as Reggie suddenly started over toward them. The youth weaved slightly.

"Who are you workin' for, Carson?" he demanded. "I see you sittin' here chawin' with one of Gruber's men, makes me wonder."

Wes leaned back in his chair. "Why don't you join us?"

"I don't sit down with killers."

"Rio Grange was an Army scout, just like me."

Reggie put a hand on the back of a chair to steady himself. "Yeah, well, I heard plenty about 'im, and I say he's a killer."

The youth's dark eyes were glassy; his right fingers played with his right holster. He was wearing a fancy blue shirt and leather vest, and his hat was pushed back.

"Sit down," Wes said, "before you fall down."

Reggie was angered. He straightened, backing away, just as Haney came in the door. The foreman didn't hesitate and came quickly forward.

"Reggie, your pa needs you out at the ranch."

Standing uncertainly, Reggie rested his hands on his six-guns. "I ain't movin' till that man apologizes."

Wes smiled. "I apologize."

Reggie was surprised and still trying to concentrate on Wes's response as Haney marshaled him out the door into the night. They could hear squabbling and Reggie's cussing. After a few moments, they heard hoofbeats.

Wes shook his head. "Somethin's eatin' that boy."

"He don't like you much."

Wes changed the subject to the Southwest and the Indian campaigns. "I was on my way north about the time they started that hot-pursuit deal with Mexico. But I heard about Seiber's being named Chief of Scouts. He was a good man. Did you follow the Army down to the Sierra Madre?"

Rio nodded. "That was a bloody trip. Pack mules falling hundreds of feet from the cliffs. Hot as the devil in the daytime and cold at night. And I was right surprised when Geronimo surrendered. Kinda killed off the old days, you know?"

"Don't sell 'im short. He may be out again."

"You got a point. He's got plenty of reason not to wanta be herded like cattle on his own land."

Wes leaned back, studying the man. "So why are you working for Gruber?"

"The pay is good. But they found gold in Alaska, you know. Place called Juneau. Maybe I'll take my poke and head up there."

"Don't figure you'd like the cold winters."

"Maybe you're right. I got me a few miseries. But things are goin' to pot around here, what with women havin' the vote down in Wyoming. I figure Alaska's got a fresh start."

"You got somethin' against women?"

"Yeah. I had four wives, and they near drove me crazy."

Wes laughed. "Four wives?"

"I outlived 'em all, and that's a wonder." Then Rio sobered. "I figure I know enough about you to trust you with somethin'. Only other one I told was the sheriff. The longer I work for the Grubers, the more suspicious I get."

"About what?"

Rio glanced around the room and lowered his voice. "I ain't sure, but I don't figure they come by their money like honest men, and they sure ain't much good at ranchin'. They act more like raw-hiders. The sheriff sent queries down to the Texas Rangers, but they have nothin' on 'em."

Wes pushed his hat back. "Go on."

"That's all I got. Call it instinct. But I tell you, Wes, men like that don't change. Sooner or later, they're gonna show their colors."

"Holler if you need help."

"Thanks." Rio stood up, glancing around the room, and he spoke softly. "Don't turn your back, Wes."

Then the man was gone, and Wes, listening to

him ride away in the night, wondered about the Grubers and just how right Rio might be. Wes had another cup of coffee, knowing he was making himself a target. Yet he knew no other way. He could see that it was dark outside, and Rio's warning only echoed what he knew.

He stood up and walked toward the swinging doors, keeping his eye on the men watching him. Then he exited and moved away from the light. It was a dark, cold night with no moon and only the stars to guide him.

He moved from the boardwalk and around the railing, reaching for the reins of the nervous stallion. He swung into the saddle.

Shots rang out from the roof of the saloon. Bullets whistled by his ear and shoulder. He spun his mount and dived from the saddle, hitting the dirt and rolling under the rail, onto the boardwalk and against the outside wall of the saloon, underneath the roof overhang.

He held his breath, waiting and listening. Six-gun in hand, he could hear the sudden silence of the saloon and no sound from the roof.

## Chapter Four

Wes pressed against the wall in front of the saloon. He saw a light go on inside the jail across the street. At that moment, he heard scrambling on the roof. Minutes later, he could hear hoofbeats echoing into the night. Then silence.

The door of the jail opened, and he straightened, taking a deep breath. He caught up his stallion and walked over in the mud.

There was a chunky man in the doorway, outlined against the lamplight. As Wes approached, he saw that the lawman was in his red underwear and scratching, but wearing a six-gun.

"What's goin' on?" the lawman grunted.

"Someone just tried to bushwhack me."

Wes tied his horse to the railing and followed the man inside. He stood with the door closed behind him as the sheriff pulled on his britches and his boots. The man had a hooked nose and large mouth, and his scraggly hair fell down over his pale eyes.

"I'm Will Perryman. You that feller what outdrew Sal Gruber and killed him?"

"Wes Carson."

"This country's runnin' with the likes of you."

"Not with the likes of me."

The sheriff pulled on his hat. "That so?"

"You got any idea who killed Randy Hollis? Or one of the men over in Turkey Creek?"

"What's it to you?"

"I'm working for Hollis."

"Figures. Listen, I got a job to do. I gotta see if them fellers are still around."

"I heard 'em ride off. That coffee hot?"

The sheriff nodded and sat down at his desk while Wes poured some coffee and sat near him. They studied each other. Perryman was obviously no gunfighter, but he had huge hands and a mean face.

The lawman leaned back. "You knew Randy?"

"No."

"Well, I can't tell you much. When I heard what happened, I went out there. The signs were mostly kicked over or dusted. Tracks of one horse, but only a couple of prints, which I couldn't see clear."

"Not much to go on."

"I know. And when I went out to Turkey Creek where old Joe was killed, I found the body of an old man down in a gully, covered with rocks. He'd been shot. Nobody knows who he was. Looked like some old prospector passin' through. Maybe they just wanted his poke, whoever done it. But there was nothin' up there to go on, either.''

Wes downed his coffee and slowly got to his feet. "I was told there's a price on my head, thanks to Ma Gruber. You gonna do anything about that?''

"You got any proof?''

Wes was grim as he considered this, and he decided, one, that he didn't want anyone to know it was Rio who had told him, and two, this man probably wouldn't do anything about it, anyhow. Yet Rio had found something trustworthy in the man, and Wes hoped he was misjudging him.

Turning, Wes pulled his hat down tight. He walked to the door, then paused as the sheriff stood up and came forward.

"Listen to me, Carson. I was a lawman in Kansas for many a year. Came here to retire in this job. You start stirrin' things up and ruinin' my peace and quiet, I ain't gonna like it much.''

"Hollis is still havin' trouble with rustlers.''

"I can't be ridin' herd on their cows. I'm only one man.''

Wes went back outside and stood in the darkness against the jail. Everything looked quiet and peaceful. No one had come outside because of the shots.

He figured everyone was either afraid or knew there was a price on his head.

He decided to head back to the Little River H, even though it was after dark. It was near midnight when he arrived, and the main house had no lights. Maybe Hollis wasn't going to let Angela see him, but then if she was going to marry someone else, it didn't matter much.

He was so weary he went right to sleep. In the morning, he was eating with the men, liking every one of them.

Haney came to sit with him. ''Mr. Hollis wants us to come up to the house.''

''You doin' anythin' special tonight?''

''Boys was gonna get out the guitars and do some singin', I reckon. And I was gonna play my harmonica. Why?''

''Seems like Mrs. Taylor's invited us both to supper tonight, around sunset. You figure you can make it?''

Haney was surprised and suddenly looked ten years younger. The man swallowed hard, then nodded, and soon he was grinning, his eyes twinkling as he said, ''Never in a million years would I have figured that. Reckon I'd better take a bath.''

A little later, when Wes and Haney entered the plush living room of the ranch house with its leather furniture, Wes could see Angela's touch. Doilies and fancy curtains and fine paintings clashed with the deer antlers and hides.

The Mexican woman, Hollis's housekeeper, brought them coffee and muffins. A fire was glowing in the hearth. Hollis was lounging in a leather chair with one leg crossed over his knee. Reggie was standing near the fireplace, looking as cocky and arrogant as before, his mouth twisted in a crooked smile, but he looked as if he had one bad headache.

There was no sign of Angela. Wes breathed easier.

Reed Hollis leaned forward, anxious. "What have you found out, Wes?" he asked.

As briefly as possible, Wes recounted his visit to the Taylors, his meeting the gunmen, and his encounter with the wolves. He then added that he had been shot at in town, had learned there was a price on his head, and had met the sheriff.

Hollis tugged at his thick red mustache. "You've sure been busy. And I reckon Perryman's all right."

"He's a coward," Reggie said, his hands on his guns.

"Ain't you got some ridin' to do?" Reed asked his son.

His stance still cocky, Reggie looked down at Wes. "The sheriff and everybody else may be afraid of you, Carson, but you don't worry me none."

"Carson's on our side," his father reminded him.

The youth stood over Wes with curled lips. Then he took out his smokes, swaggered his way to the door, and went outside, leaving Reed Hollis frowning.

"When my wife died, she made me promise to be patient with that boy."

Haney folded his arms. "He'll be all right, Mr. Hollis. He was just in his brother's shadow for so long, he's tryin' to take his place. He'll settle down."

The rancher turned to Wes. "You oughta stick around here awhile. Let 'em come to you. Might give you an edge. And you bein' here, maybe they'll even stay away."

It was then that Wes caught his breath, sensing the presence of Angela. He turned slowly to see her coming down the stairs in a bright blue dress, her hair done in the same large curls, her smile casual and bright, dimples flashing, as if she and Wes had never spoken cross words.

Wes watched her as he and Haney got to their feet.

*Strange,* he thought, *my heart isn't racing.* Memory came forth from five years ago and rested on her pretty face, but there was no pain. And now he realized why. It was as if he were meeting her for the first time. He kind of liked it that way, starting over. She wasn't twenty anymore. She was a serene, smiling woman, almost a stranger.

"Wes Carson," she said, extending her hand, "you haven't changed."

He swallowed hard, but lamely shook her hand. He felt numb, his knees buckling. Then he backed away, glancing at Haney for help.

"Well," Haney said, "I reckon we got some ridin' to do, Wes. Gonna show you the spread."

Angela was miffed. "But it's been five years. I want to talk with Wes."

"Later," her father said.

Wes quickly took up his hat and followed Haney outside. He was relieved to be in the fresh air, away from Angela.

"You all right?" Haney grunted.

Wes nodded, surprised that he was. And now it irked him that she had sent for him because of the very skills she disliked.

The day was spent trailing the edge of the spread up the river and then cutting across center. There wasn't time to go to Turkey Creek, but Haney assured him it was a canyon about ten miles wide, spread with rich green grass and a sparkling creek.

It was late afternoon when Haney and Wes returned to the ranch to get ready for their Sunday dinner at the Taylors'. Both took baths and spruced up, making the other hands laugh.

At twilight, they reached the river ford where Randy Hollis had been murdered. There on the opposite bank were three riders. On each side were two men in their thirties who looked more like cowhands than gunmen, their clothes as weathered as their faces, but in the center was the Brazos Kid.

Brazos was young and angry and arrogant. He loosened his red bandanna and pushed back his Stetson, his small dark eyes gleaming. "You lookin' for me, Carson?" he asked, his voice hoarse.

"Not likely."

"Are you ready to face me like a man this time?"

"What for?"

"Well, now, they been sayin' how you're the fastest there is. I don't believe you beat Sal Gruber fair and square, and I aim to prove it, here and now."

Wes sat grim in the saddle. He was wearing his only clean shirt and britches. He had even scraped and polished his boots. His wide-brimmed hat was brushed, and his bandanna had been washed. He didn't want to tangle with Brazos, but he wasn't going to avoid it.

Haney leaned on the pommel and tugged at his mustache. "Listen here, Brazos, if you wanta be buzzard bait, go ahead. Carson draws so fast, you can't see his hand move."

"Is that a fact? Swanson and Miller here, they took a few shots at him in town and missed. Let me tell you, mister, I don't miss."

Brazos was sneering, his thin body erect in the saddle as his bay pawed the soft earth near the water. The two men with him looked a little nervous, and abruptly, they both reined back and away from the gunman, who was amused.

"Don't worry, Carson, I don't need no help."

Wes didn't respond.

"Look at it this way," Brazos said, "if you wanta cross this river onto Gruber land, you gotta go through me."

Wes started his horse toward the water, which was about three feet deep on a sandy bottom. Powerful muscles moving, the stallion forced its way into the current.

Wes felt sweat trickling down his back. His mouth was tight and dry. Heat burned his skin from the inside out, and his heart was pounding.

Brazos was stiff in the saddle, his hand near his six-gun. Wes kept coming, and Brazos remembered how it had been before. He wasn't waiting for any tricks.

Suddenly, Brazos drew his six-gun and aimed, but before he could pull the trigger, he was staring at Wes's Colt. Frightened, Brazos squeezed to fire, but the bullet from Wes's gun whistled into the gunman's chest, dead center. Brazos fired his gun, missing as his free hand clutched the sudden rush of blood.

For a moment, the gunman was suspended in the saddle, and then he fell sideways like a sack of grain, his boots caught in the stirrups as his horse jumped. And then he jerked crazily, grasping the pommel with all his remaining strength. His six-gun slid from his hand and crashed down into the mud.

Frantic, he leaned down, trying to reach for it. Then he crumpled up and fell from the saddle, his left foot caught in the stirrup. His horse shied, jerking its head, but didn't run away.

Wes felt the same sickness in his belly whenever he had to kill a man. Sweat was soaking the back of his shirt.

One of the cowhands came forward and held the reins of the dead gunman's horse, while the other dismounted to kneel over the body. The cowhand hesitated, then stood up and spoke to Wes, who was riding out of the water, Colt still in hand.

"Old man Gruber and his other sons will be back tonight. If I was you, I'd head out mighty fast."

Wes leaned back in the saddle. "So it was you boys who took a shot at me."

Their faces were suddenly run with sweat as they stared at the gun in Wes's hand. One put both hands on the saddle horn as he spoke.

"We was just doin' what we was told. You don't say no to a Gruber. They're the meanest bunch you ever saw. And Ma Gruber's the toughest."

Wes shrugged and holstered his gun, remembering Rio's words, that the Grubers could be outlaws— men who could kill without hesitation—passing themselves off as ranchers.

Haney rode into the water and crossed, watching

the cowhands dismount to tie Brazos onto the saddle. Wes and Haney waited until the men were mounted and riding away with Brazos trailing.

Haney pushed his hat back. "You're the fastest I've seen, Wes, but if you're smart, you won't stick around."

"I ain't turnin' tail."

They rode on, the wind in their faces, and they crossed the meadowland. It was dark now; a full moon hung in the sky, guiding them. Stars were spread like diamonds.

"Biggest sky in the West," Haney remarked.

When they sighted the lights in the Taylor ranch house, Haney reined up and removed his hat. He smoothed his hair, then used his bandanna to wipe his face.

"Maybe she was just bein' nice, Wes. Maybe I'm just there counta you."

"You look so darn pretty, she'll be all over you."

Haney swallowed hard. "Ain't easy, an old cowhand like me. I mean I don't know nothin' except bein' in the saddle. What if she sets out all them little forks and spoons?"

"There ain't nothin' a woman likes better than to show a man his manners, so don't you worry."

But Haney *was* worried, and as they rode on, he wiped his face again. When they dismounted and approached the door, Haney was plenty nervous. Wes had to do the knocking.

The door opened, framing Clarisa in the lamplight. Her dark, gray-streaked hair was set in waves about her face, and she looked pretty. In fact, she looked ten years younger than the day before. She was wearing a blue print dress with a high collar.

Hats in their hands, Haney and Wes moved inside. A fire was aglow in the hearth. Taylor was getting around better and was happy to see them. Cindy was wearing a full apron over her green dress, limping around and fussing over supper, but she sure looked pretty with flour on her nose.

Haney told them right out about Brazos. "And that's one less killer on the prowl. Swanson and Miller lit out, probably couldn't wait to get back to tell the Grubers."

Taylor nodded approval to Wes. "You're a blessin', son."

Wes glanced at Cindy, wondering if she would see him as a killer, the way Angela did, but Cindy was smiling. Her red hair glistened in the lamplight.

Supper was a great success, with lively conversation. Clarisa had roasted a fat rooster with dressing and potatoes. Fluffy biscuits and jelly rounded out the meal. The men ate so much they could hardly breathe. The little dog, which slept most of the time, often looked up to keep his eye on Wes.

Haney turned to Cindy. "I was wonderin' where you got your red hair."

Clarisa smiled, touching the gray in her auburn

hair. "My hair was light red when I was young, and my mother's was fire red. She was Irish, and what a temper."

Wes grinned. "So that's why your daughter's so quick on the trigger."

Cindy merely smiled, while Clarisa flirted with Haney, who was floating on a cloud all evening. The foreman was even brave enough to play his harmonica as they sat around the fire. In sweet, clear voices, Cindy and Clarisa sang everything from "Amazing Grace" to "Red River Valley."

It was near midnight when the little dog suddenly jumped up from its spot near the blazing fire. It growled and ran to the front door. It barked, then scratched at the wood and ran in circles.

"Scotty, be quiet," Cindy scolded gently.

Wes quickly got to his feet and hurried over to the window, sliding the wooden shutter aside a crack as Haney blew out the lamp. The women tried to shield the light from the hearth as Wes shaded his eyes and peered outside. He could hear horses somewhere in the night.

Anxious, Taylor hobbled over to gather up his big rifle. "Ain't been no Injun trouble since the Nez Percé come through in '77."

Haney moved over, next to Wes. "I heard rumors Sitting Bull was comin' down from Canada."

The little dog was snarling, his hair standing on end.

Wes peered into the night and was startled as bright fire shot upward from the barn. He could see riders circling it, and now they were firing into the air.

He sprang to the door and unbarred it, then drew his six-gun. He and Haney jumped outside and away from the light from the doorway. The five riders were yelling and shooting, framed now and then by the blazing fire.

Wes fired, hitting one in the shoulder.

Surprised, the riders spun their horses and fired back. Haney was hit in the thigh. Wes fired again and got one man in the arm. The men jerked their horses about and headed into the night, their hoofbeats fading in the roar of the fire.

Wes started for his stallion, then thought better of it and turned to the frantic Taylor. "Any animals in there?"

"No, just the hay we cut for winter."

Haney, leaning on the wall of the house, was gripping his thigh and shaking his head. "It's gone now, Mr. Taylor."

They stood staring as the barn burned so fast there was no way to save it. Flames ate the walls and roof, made searing hot by the hay burning inside.

"All that work," Taylor muttered.

"Well, Wes hit two of 'em," Haney said. "Maybe we'll take a ride over to Gruber's and have a look."

"You ain't goin' nowhere," Taylor told him. "Get inside."

Clarisa came to help Haney hobble inside, but Wes headed for the barn and Cindy followed him. It was cold until they were within fifty feet of the structure. Then the blazing heat forced them to stop. No corrals or other structures were in danger, nor were there any animals at risk. But Cindy was devastated.

"Oh, Wes! It just isn't fair."

"Well, you got a couple of months to get in some more hay. Maybe you could have a barn raising."

"No one will help us now. They're afraid of the Grubers."

Side by side, they circled the barn, making sure there was no way for the fire to spread. Most of the ground around the structure was mud and drainage from the corral. It was wet and well trodden by cattle. There was no grass within fifty feet, and there was no wind.

Weary, Cindy sat on the edge of the trough by the corral. The horses, at the far end, were nervous. Her little dog lay at her feet as she reached down to rub her sore foot.

Wes leaned on the fence, watching the barn collapse until there was nothing left but fiery embers.

"Wes, what can we do to make them leave us alone?"

"I don't know."

"Next time, my grandfather could be killed. Or my mother."

"Or you."

"No, nothing ever happens to me."

"Except wolves."

She smiled and started to rise, and Wes came forward to take her right hand and pull her to her feet. The little dog growled and ran around them.

Cindy looked up at Wes, her eyes glistening. He stood there holding her hand, his heart racing crazily in his chest. She reached up with her left hand to touch his face. He could hear his own breath. His brow was damp, and he pushed his hat back.

"I'm glad you're here," she whispered.

Wes couldn't help himself. A beautiful woman was touching his face and standing so close he could smell the lilacs.

He drew her into his arms and lifted her so that he could bend to kiss her cool, sweet lips. She slid her hand to his neck, and this time he wasn't thinking of Angela. His lips caressed hers gently. She kissed him back.

The little dog barked and growled and bit at Wes's boot. Cindy drew back, laughing, and Wes released her while he shook his foot. The dog seized his trouser leg and held on, growling.

"Scotty," she scolded, "Wes is our friend."

The dog finally let go as she backed away. He sat on his rear and looked up at Wes, barking twice.

Wes pulled his hat down and glared down at the animal, then had to laugh.

To the dog's surprise, Wes suddenly bent down and grabbed it around the belly, holding it under his arm as it struggled and growled and bit at the air. Then Wes rubbed it behind the ears and watched as it struggled to get free.

Wes finally set it down, and it backed away, barking once, then sniffing Wes's boot and spur before running on ahead. Wes and Cindy headed back toward the house, where they found Clarisa fussing over Haney's wounded thigh, the foreman loving every minute of it.

"We'll stay until morning," Wes said.

Haney didn't protest. He was bleeding, but he couldn't take his gaze off Clarisa. His growing affection for her was written all over his face. Wes thought it comical and hoped he never looked that silly.

## Chapter Five

Silas Gruber was a wiry, whiskered, graying man with the same hawklike face and dark eyes as his sons, but with more energy and drive than they had. He paced the front room while the fire blazed in the stone hearth. Hides hung on the walls and covered the floor. The leather furniture was worn and faded. Near the entrance a gun case held several rifles.

"I was gone only a month," Silas growled. "Now you tell me we lost Sal to some hired gun."

Seth was sitting near the far wall, close to the lantern on the table. He was playing with a deck of cards, silent and fearful.

Simon and Sloan, the older brothers, were seated in leather chairs, sipping their coffee. They wore leather vests and fancy silver spurs with jingle bobs, and their holsters were tied down.

"Look, Pa," Seth said, straightening, "that Wes Carson was just askin' for it. He was embarrassin' Sal in front of the town, pullin' him off that Taylor girl, hittin' him with his fist when he wasn't lookin'. Sal had to stand up to him."

Silas folded his arms. "So we lost Sal over a fool woman. And riled up the town, I expect. I told you before and I'll tell you again. If we don't have the town and the law behind us, we can't get nothin' done."

It was then that Martha Gruber came into the room. She wiped her hands on her apron as she looked firmly at her husband.

"Now, Silas," she said, her lips tight and thin, "you're being too hard. Ain't nobody in this valley worth spittin' on but these boys, and you know it."

"Martha, you stay out of this."

"I ain't stayin' out of it. They're my boys too. Now, Sal was old enough to take care of himself, and it's a sorry thing we lost 'im. But we're settin' things right. We sent Brazos over there to get rid of Carson."

"We'll see," Silas grunted. "Meanwhile, we're goin' back to Turkey Creek without the law behind us. What I learned in Butte don't make sense at all, but seems there's gotta be a district marked off by everyone around, and claims assigned, and a recorder, and water apportioned out, and a miner's court formed just to tell you how long you have to work on a claim to keep it, and all that foolishness."

Martha stared at him. "You ain't makin' sense."

"That's what I said," Silas growled. "But that's the way it is. All that gold in Bannack and Virginia City, and up in Helena and over in Missoula. Fellow said that's how they get started when there's a strike. 'Counta there ain't no way to keep it secret."

"What fellow?" she asked.

"Marcus Daly," Simon told her. "But I ain't so sure he knows what he's talkin' about. I mean, here's a fool in country run with gold and tickled with silver, and what's he gonna do? Mine copper!"

Martha was amused. "Copper? That's for pots and pans."

Silas grimaced. "I don't care nothin' about them crazy people. All I want is to find that gold in Turkey Creek. It's near pure. We'd never have to work again, once we got it out. And since we can't get it legal like, we'll just take it."

"Simon and me, we shoulda let that old prospector live long enough to take us to his diggin's," Sloan said, lighting a smoke. "But Simon, he lost his temper. Even shot the old man's dog."

"Killed 'em both," Simon growled. "But we got the gold he was carryin', didn't we? Four sacks. And he did admit to gettin' it out of Turkey Creek Meadows. He was just too ornery to say where it was. Wasn't my fault he wouldn't talk."

Sloan nodded. "The way we rolled him and the dog into a gully and rolled rocks over 'em, no one will ever find 'im. So no one suspects anything. All we got to do is keep Hollis outa there."

Martha frowned, folding her arms. "I sure hope we do, 'cause this ranchin' ain't no pleasure. It's all right for you men out there where the action is, but I'm sick and tired of tryin' to be respectable."

Silas grunted and took a chaw of tobacco. "Well, Martha, you put on a good show, just the same. I like the way you hold your head up when we go to church."

"That's another thing," Sloan said. "I get real nervous when you drag us there. Next time, I ain't goin'."

They were interrupted by a pounding on the door. Seth went to peer through the window, then unbarred the door and let in a cowhand in a heavy coat.

"All right, Miller, what do you want?" Silas asked.

"Well, uh, Mr. Gruber, me and Swanson and Brazos, we went to cross the river and, uh, we was huntin' that Wes Carson."

Martha came to her husband's side, her face brightening. "And so?"

Miller pushed his hat back and shrugged. "Well, uh, we run into Carson and that feller Haney at the river, all right. Brazos, he called Carson out, and— well, Carson beat 'im to the draw and shot him dead center. Swanson, he took Brazos over to the barn. We'll bury him come mornin'.''

Martha's face darkened with anger, and Silas thanked the man, ushering him out and barring the door.

''Silas, we done all we could. Now it's your turn,'' Martha told her husband.

Silas was uneasy. ''I figure we oughta do our own fightin', all right, but I just don't like Carson workin' for Hollis. And if he could take Brazos, we have to go easy.''

''He's only one man,'' she said.

''But it means Hollis wants to fight, and I was figurin' on gettin' that gold without any more trouble.''

Hands on hips, she glared at him. ''Don't you back down on me now. We gotta get rid of Carson.''

Seth spoke up. ''Maybe Chuck Maddox can take 'im.''

The rancher sat down, his face grim. His wife came to his side, suddenly smiling and kneeling by his chair, her hand on his arm.

''I'm sorry, Silas. It's just that we have the boys to think about. They'll be wantin' to marry one day, but when you divide what we got, there isn't much to go around. Hollis doesn't own all that land. He just sits on it. And he did pull out of Turkey Creek after Simon killed that man of his, so maybe he won't go back.''

Sloan stoked the fire, then asked, ''What about the Taylors, Ma?''

''If we let 'em stay, there'll be more movin' in. I hate them squatters. But I wouldn't mind gettin' some of them fat chickens some night.''

''Some of the boys are burnin' their barn tonight,'' Seth said. ''The old man is crippled. They won't hold out much longer. But I wouldn't mind bringin' that Cindy home.''

Sloan laughed. ''She's too much woman for you, boy.''

While the Grubers argued into the night, Reed Hollis was at his house, sitting in front of his own hearth while Maria served coffee. He smiled at Angela as she leaned back on the couch. Then he turned to his son, who was slumped in a chair nearby.

''Reggie, you're drinkin' too much.''

''Just when I think about Randy.''

''Your brother never drank.''

''No, but he's dead.''

''You know we're expectin' trouble with the Grubers. I need you to have your head on straight.''

''Pa, I ain't worried about the Grubers. But you oughta be worried about Carson. I seen him in town talkin' with one of Gruber's gunhands. You had your eye on Turkey Creek Meadows. You wanted to build over there. And you let Carson have it.''

''I gave my word, yes.''

"Well, it just might be that he won't be around to collect. If the Grubers don't take him, maybe I will."

Reed Hollis leaned back in his chair, crossing one leg over his knee, fingertips together, staring into the fire as he shielded his disappointment over this young son. He thought sadly of his wife, who had died so young, and of the many promises he had made her.

And he thought of his older son, Randy, and of the way he had died down by the river. He had vowed to find the killers, but he knew he had no way to do so.

All he had left now was a vast spread, an arrogant young son, and a daughter who chose men she could handle, men who would do her bidding.

"Pa, your problem is you ain't never seen the man I am. Maybe with Randy gone, you'll start lookin' at me for a change. I'm fast, Pa. And I can ride any bronc you throw at me. And the men don't talk back to me."

"I hope you're right, son."

"You'll see I'm right. And I'll get them rustlers for you. You don't need Carson for that. And I'll get the ones that killed Randy."

"How you plannin' to do that?"

"First off, I'm gonna run some cattle up to Turkey Creek."

"I already gave that to Carson."

"Don't matter. He ain't usin' it, and when I run the cattle up there, I'll get them rustlers. I'll hide some men in the brush and just wait for 'em."

"You know we got no gun hands."

"Some were friends with the man we lost, so they'll be willin'. You let me handle it, Pa."

While Reggie continued to rave about how he would solve everything for the Little River H, Angela was lost in thoughts and memories surrounding Wes Carson. She could still feel his arms about her that night in Fort Apache, could see his sudden embarrassment when she had refused him. She wondered if she could finally make him do her bidding.

In the morning, Wes and Haney prepared to leave the Taylor spread. Clarisa was fussing over Haney's bandaged thigh, and she made sure he had a sackful of cookies.

Outside, both women stood with Taylor and watched Wes help Haney into the saddle. As Wes started to mount, he glanced toward the ruins of the hay barn. Then he looked at Cindy, with the little dog at her side. It was growling at him every time he moved.

She smiled up at him. "Please be careful, Wes."

"Just keep your dog off me," he said, grinning.

"You know, I've figured it out. He doesn't like your spurs."

"That a fact?"

Wes considered this, and to humor her, he reached down and took off his spurs, handing them to her. He then turned and looked down at the dog. It was growling and watching him intently as Wes walked casually around him, no spurs to jingle.

Wes knelt and reached out his hands. The dog stopped growling and suddenly lay down. Wes moved closer, and the dog bit at him but not viciously. Wes rubbed the dog behind the ears, and then he lifted it in his arms. It struggled briefly and then was quiet. Wes scratched its neck, and it licked his hand.

"Well, I'll be," Taylor said. "Cindy, you're right."

"He must have a reason," Cindy said, thoughtful.

Wes agreed, and he turned to her. "You keep my spurs for me, for luck."

Color flushed her face, and she looked very pleased. Wes felt awkward as he turned to his stallion and mounted.

When they were out of sight of the ranch, Haney began to complain about his thigh, but Wes kept thinking what a fool thing he had done, leaving his spurs with Cindy. He wondered if he had done it to tie him to some woman other than Angela, in self-protection.

Back at the ranch, he went to the house with Haney, who hobbled up the steps with Wes's help. Reggie had just ridden up, and he followed them inside. Haney slumped in a chair, and Wes sat near him. Reggie stood by, glaring. There was no sign of Angela.

With great detail, Haney told Reed Hollis of the fight with Brazos. "I tell you, Mr. Hollis, by the time this is over, Gruber won't have no more gun hands," he finished.

The rancher was more concerned about Haney's wound. "Never mind that. Right now, I want you taken into town. Wes, you wait right here. Come on, Haney, let's get someone to hitch the wagon. I want the doc to look you over."

Wes watched them leave, then stood at the window, impressed as he saw the way Hollis fussed over Haney and got him into a wagon, which one of the men was driving.

"Wes, I'm glad we're alone."

Startled, he turned to see Angela coming from another room. She was wearing a blue dress with a white shawl, and she sure looked pretty. He felt awkward, cornered.

"I'm sorry about what happened down at Fort Apache," she said softly. "I was afraid of you. Did you know that?"

"Well, I—"

"You were so wild and wore those terrible buckskins. And you always seemed to have blood on you."

"Well, uh, not anymore."

She moved closer. "But you still hire out your gun."

"Not exactly. I was workin' for the stock growers."

"Same thing."

Now she was inches from contact, her lips parted, blue eyes soft and shining. He remembered how he had loved her and wanted to marry her. Afraid to touch, he backed against the window.

"I hear you're gettin' married," he said.

"I just can't seem to marry anyone since I met you."

"This Cliff Sellers, I hear he's a gentleman."

She came up against him, her hands sliding up his chest. He swallowed hard, unable to move. She stood on her tiptoes and slid a hand around his neck, pulling his head down.

And now she was kissing him. His heart went cold.

When she drew back, she was staring up at him. "You didn't kiss me back."

He moved around and away from her, adjusting his hat and glancing toward the door. "It's been a long time, Angela."

"But you loved me."

"It's been five years."

"You're still angry at me, is that it? Just because I didn't want to stay in that old fort while you played soldier?"

"You said I was a dirty, sweaty killer with no manners and no decency and that I'd never amount to anything."

"I was only trying to get you to quit."

She moved toward him again, and he moved away, toward the door, his hand on the latch just as it opened. Reed Hollis came in and paused, seeing how flushed his daughter was and the way Wes was so nervous.

"Sit with me, Wes," Hollis said.

Angela was miffed at the interruption and went up to her room. Hollis and Wes sat down and had fresh coffee that Maria served.

"It's Reggie," the rancher said. "He insisted on taking some cattle and men back to Turkey Creek to set an ambush for the rustlers."

Wes was still unsettled because of Angela. He leaned back and sipped his coffee without answering.

"I know it's your place, Wes, but you got to know Reggie's not easy to handle. He was always jealous of Randy, even though I tried to treat 'em alike. It was just that Randy had a lot more sense and was evenhanded. So I'm askin' you not to try to stop 'im."

"I reckon he can't hurt the place none."

"Good. And he'll be sittin' up there for weeks, waiting for someone to show. Maybe it'll calm him down some. He'll get impatient and come on home.

Now, what about the Taylors? I don't like what's happenin' over there. I respect that old man, even if he is a squatter. Can we help 'em any?''

"It's a far piece to keep an eye on 'em."

Just then, there was a knock on the door. Hollis got up and went over to jerk it open. Standing there were Pete and the sheriff, blood all over the lawman's chest.

## Chapter Six

Pete helped the sheriff inside Hollis's house, and the rancher put his arm around the wounded man. Wes helped them half carry him to the couch, where he lay back, his hand on his chest, his eyes half closed.

"What happened?" Hollis asked.

"I was upriver. I come across the Grubers with a dozen of your cows. They throwed down on me afore I knew what they was up to. They left me for dead."

"You're bleedin' bad," Hollis said, beckoning to Maria at the same time. "We'll clean you up, get you to town. A few inches to the right, you'd have been dead—I guess you know that."

Maria brought in a kettle of hot water and some

towels. As she worked on the man's chest wound, Hollis knelt close.

"Which of the Grubers was it?"

Perryman coughed, his eyes dazed. "It was Sloan and that younger one, Seth. It was Sloan who drew first. Didn't even see his hand move. When they pushed me in the river, I heard 'em laughing. But when they was gone, I dragged myself out, and my horse was still there. Stuck my arm through the stirrup and hung on."

"It's a wonder you ain't dead," Pete said.

Hollis turned to the cowhand. "Get a wagon ready and take this man to town."

"First Randy," Pete said, "and old Joe up at Turkey Creek, then Haney takes a bullet, and now this." Then he turned around and went outside.

Wes sat watching Maria bandaging the lawman's wound. He had a little more respect for Perryman now. It took guts to hang on to a stirrup for miles, guts to stay alive, and the man was barely that.

Angela came into the room. Her eyes widened when she saw the bloody shirt on the arm of the couch, and she turned her face away. Maria went to her and took her hand.

Hearing the wagon outside, Wes and the rancher helped the weakened lawman to his feet. Then they formed a chair with their arms, lifted him, and carried him outside. The man had lost a lot of blood but was still coherent.

"Carson, I'm gonna deputize you," he said as they put him in the wagon. He pulled off his own star and held it out it to Wes, who stared at it.

"Go on, take it. Rio trusts you. So do I."

The lawman's words were startling but pleasing. Despite his inner warnings, Wes took the star.

Perryman lay back, gazing up at Wes anxiously. "You bring in them two Grubers—alive."

Hollis frowned. "This is crazy, Will. One man can't do that."

The sheriff coughed and said, "Carson can." Then he lay back, closing his eyes. They covered him with blankets, wondering if he was going to live. Pete set the wagon moving and headed toward town.

Wes and Hollis stood watching the wagon until it disappeared from sight. Then Wes looked down at the silver star in his hand. It was a strange sight, and he wasn't sure why he had taken it. Uneasy, he hooked it on his double-breasted shirt.

Hollis cleared his throat. "I'll go with you. And I'll leave word for the men when they ride in, to see if some of 'em will go along."

"How many men went with Reggie?"

Hollis turned pale. "Three."

"I figure we'd better have a look up there."

Hollis started running toward the corral, and Wes

followed. They saddled and headed out together, the stallion far ahead of Hollis's bay. Wes had to hold back to get directions, and within two hours, they saw a red-streaked cliff near the river. Rounding it, they were in the meadows.

Turkey Creek was several feet deep and swift with white water. The afternoon sun glistened on the spray as they crossed over and turned north across sweet, deep grass dotted with wildflowers. It was a grand sight for a cattleman.

Soon they saw a few head of cattle grazing in the trees. The rustlers had either missed them or the cows were too wild to handle. There was no sign of Reggie or the three cowhands.

Slowly, they rode along the creek, watching through the cottonwoods. Then they saw a man face-down in the water. Wes swung down and pulled the cowhand onto the grass, but he was dead.

''Blast!'' Hollis muttered.

Wes swung back into the saddle, and they moved on, watching carefully, but nearly riding over the bodies of two more men along the creek. Hollis was sweating now, and he looked around anxiously.

They rode another few hundred yards, and they heard something crawling through the brush by the creek. Six-guns drawn, they approached, and Hollis called out.

''Reggie?''

''Pa,'' came a whine.

Hollis swung down and ran to the brush as his son came crawling out, his head and neck dark with blood. Frantic, Hollis knelt and cradled him against his knee.

"Pa, we were layin' for 'em," Reggie gasped. "But they sneaked up on us instead. When they got me, I played possum."

"The other three men are dead, son."

"I figured, but I was out for a while. I couldn't move. When I come to, they were gone, but they'd run off with our horses."

Hollis was grim. "See who they were?"

"Sloan Gruber and his little brother, Seth."

"Did you hit any of 'em?"

"I don't know, Pa."

Reggie blinked his eyes, his color slowly returning. He couldn't sit up without his father's help. He'd been creased on the side of his head but he had somehow survived.

Hollis used his bandanna to wipe some of the blood from Reggie's face, then looked up at Wes. "Help me get my son in the saddle."

Once Reggie was up on Hollis's horse, the rancher swung up behind him and put his arms around him. Then he turned to Wes and said, "I'm afraid I can't go with you. I've got to get Reggie home, and I have to get my men back here for the bodies afore the varmints come."

"Don't worry," Wes told him. "I work better alone."

Hollis was hesitant. "It's two against one."

"I can take 'em, so go on. But I'll tell you this— I don't figure they was here for cattle. I'm thinkin' they took 'em to make it look that way. I figure they'll let 'em run loose."

"What else could they be after?"

"I don't know, but remember, Perryman found the body of an old prospector in a gully up here."

"I forgot about that. What have you got in mind?"

"I'm not sure, but it'd have to be easy pickin's. Them Grubers don't look like men who like to sweat."

"Listen, maybe we oughta just send for the U.S. Marshal."

"By then, they'd know Perryman and Reggie were alive and ready to testify, and they'd be lookin' to kill 'em off. No, I'm gonna pick 'em off now, one way or the other."

Hollis turned in the saddle and looked up Turkey Creek. "Your cattle will get fat here, Wes, if you live to run 'em." Then he cradled his son in his arms and headed east toward his ranch.

Wes turned south toward the river. He leaned in the saddle to look at the grass for turned blades and rocks out of their sockets. He could see the lawman's trail where his horse had dragged him. The river was wide but shallow, glistening, and clean.

Wes glanced at the rolling hills around him. A rifle could be behind any rock or cottonwood.

As he expected, a mile upstream, he found the Hollis cows grazing peacefully. The Grubers didn't want any evidence on their hands, unaware that there was a live witness.

They had tried to disguise their trail, dragging brush over the sand along the river, but Wes found little rocks out of place and bits of brush stuck in the sand. He could see where they had crossed.

As he set his stallion across the stream, he knew he could be riding into a bullet. The Grubers wouldn't hesitate to ambush him, but right now, they had to be feeling mighty confident.

He rode up into the grass, picking up their trail on the hillside. They were riding at a leisurely pace, and Wes was in no hurry. He could see they were making a wide circle, perhaps to make sure they were not followed.

It was night when he closed in on them. The two men had camped along a creek, the firelight showing them clearly. They were mighty sure of themselves.

Wes dismounted and left his stallion in the trees. He took his rifle and moved carefully, silently. He thought of how many times he had done this back in Arizona, tracking Apaches, and how often he had stalked rustlers down along the Powder River.

As he neared the campfire, he could see them

moving about. He knelt to allow a lot of silence to fall around him.

When he was certain the two men were oblivious to the world, he moved in closer. He could hear them laughing, then talking over their meal. They were wearing leather coats.

"I reckon old Hollis will start thinkin' Turkey Creek is bad luck," Sloan was saying. "He didn't pay attention the first time we got one of his men. But maybe he'll stay away from there from now on."

"We sure pulled a fast one. There they was, all hidin' in the brush. They never even heard us sneakin' up on 'em."

"All we gotta do now is find that old man's diggin's."

"I sure hope you and Simon hid his body well enough."

"Don't you worry about it. Now we've covered about one whole side of Turkey Creek. I don't figure that old man was any smarter than us, so we gotta stumble on it sooner or later."

"You know, Sloan, I sure wish you hadn't killed his dog. It might bring us bad luck."

"Well, it made me mad."

"We'd better find that mine pretty soon," Seth said. "I wasn't cut out for pushin' cows. I don't know why we even had to have all them cattle in the first place."

"You know it was the only safe way to turn that Army payroll around. Besides, Pa gets these ideas about settlin' down."

"Until you and Simon brought in that gold."

Sloan nodded, downing his coffee. "Yeah, well, it was easy money. But we can't spend that, neither. How we gonna explain two sacks of pure gold dust unless we got us a mine?"

"If we go to Oregon, nobody need ask where we got it. It's time to move on, and time to get rid of them gunmen Pa hired. Like that Chuck Maddox. Why do we need him? He gives me the willies."

"Pa knew him down in Texas. He trusts 'im."

"And what about Rio? He's always watchin' us."

Sloan shrugged. "He's fast."

It was then that Wes silently stepped into the firelight, his rifle balanced at his side with his left hand. His right hand held his six-gun, and he spoke calmly.

"Reach."

Surprised cold, they stared at him as they slowly raised their hands and stumbled to their feet. The star on his shirt glistened in the firelight.

Seth stiffened. "What do you want here, Carson?"

Sloan grimaced. "So you're the fancy gun."

"You killed some good men up on Turkey Creek, and from what I heard, you're wanted somewhere for robbin' the Army. Texas maybe?"

"That's a lie."

"Tell it to the judge."

"What, that fat Churchill?"

"Left hands, unbuckle your gunbelts."

Seth obeyed, letting his fall to the ground.

Wes lowered his rifle as he watched them. Sloan was hesitating, his eyes gleaming like hot coals.

"Why don't you come and take it, Carson?"

Wes stood calm and quiet as he considered Sloan's stance. The man was obviously unafraid to die, his hand dangling near his holster.

Apparently, Wes had two choices. He could shoot the man in cold blood or he could play the game by holstering his gun and trying to beat Sloan to the draw. But Wes looked for a third choice. Keeping his rifle on Sloan, he holstered his six-gun and started walking forward.

Startled, Sloan took a step backward.

Wes kept coming. Sloan stared into the barrel of Wes's Winchester, his mouth working and mustache twitching.

"You afraid to give me a fair chance?" Sloan demanded.

Suddenly, Wes switched the rifle around and jammed the butt hard in the man's belly. Eyes bugging, Sloan gasped in pain, breath gone, doubling up. Wes slammed his fist down on the back of the man's head, dropping him to his knees, and he grabbed Sloan's six-gun from the holster. Then he stepped back.

Sloan looked up, gasping for air, his dark eyes wild. "Blast you, Carson!" he gasped. "You're gonna pay for this."

"Seth, you tie your brother's hands behind his back with those rawhide strings off his bedroll."

Frightened, his color gone, Seth obeyed with Sloan's painful cooperation, then stepped back. Wes waved the rifle.

"Now you saddle the horses, but first, you'd better pull those rifles and lay 'em by the fire, and don't try anything."

Seth obeyed, setting the rifles aside. He was fearful and sweating, his gaze constantly darting to Wes's Winchester.

When Sloan was in the saddle, Wes tied Seth's hands behind his back and helped him swing astride. The sorrels were nervous, one pawing the earth, the other bucking a little. Wes looped one of the reins around Sloan's saddle horn, then shoved the other in the man's mouth.

"Ride in front of me, and don't try anything. Head for the river."

"But it's still dark," Seth complained. "We'll drown. And if you take us to Hollis's place, he'll try to hang us."

"And I might just let 'im."

"Then you ain't no better than us," Seth said.

"Maybe you're right, so you'd better watch it."

Wes went to Seth's horse and shoved a free rein

in Seth's mouth, the youth fighting to keep it in his teeth, his eyes blazing with hatred.

The two Grubers used their heels to move their horses. As they made their way northward, it started to rain—a cold, miserable downpour.

## Chapter Seven

Wes pulled on his leather coat while the two prisoners huddled in theirs as they rode ahead, hands tied behind their backs, reins in their teeth. Rain dribbled off their hat brims. It was icy cold.

Wes knew he would have plenty of help if he could get back across the river and over to the Hollis spread, but he was worried. He didn't like the idea of a hanging, and the cowhands had now lost four of their friends. Worse, Hollis had nearly lost his son and was fed up with the Grubers.

Wes thought morosely of Angela. He wondered what she would think now about his violent ways. She had lost one brother, and the other was badly wounded. Maybe she would be as ready to hang the Grubers as her father might be.

Heading east on the south side of the river, Wes

made his decision. He would cut through the Taylors' place and head for town. He would get across Gruber land before daylight.

But the going was slower than he had expected. His stallion handled the mud and downpour with ease, but the two sorrels the Grubers were riding kept slipping and sliding. Once Sloan almost went down. The prisoners were frantically guiding their mounts with their knees.

When daylight broke, they were on the Taylor spread. He saw some of the cattle huddled under the cottonwoods near the river, which was rising fast and furiously. The rain was still cold and heavy.

He could see a rider coming across the hills to his right, and he pulled his Winchester, reining up but letting the two men continue. Bent low in his slicker on a black horse, the man was carrying a rifle pointed downward.

Lightning flashed across the early dawn, dancing in the black clouds and touching the far bluffs. The rider kept coming. The two Grubers, realizing something was happening, urged their horses to stop.

"Now you're in for it," Sloan said, grunting from the side of his mouth and nearly losing the rein. "That's one of our men."

But as the black horse neared, the rider lifted the brim of a black hat to reveal the lovely face of Cindy Taylor.

Wes shoved his rifle back into the scabbard as she

rode up beside him. She was smiling, shivering in her slicker.

"Looks like you caught a couple of polecats."

Sloan twisted in the saddle and growled.

Cindy rested her rifle across the pommel. "Well, now, I think I'll just ride along with you, Wes, if you don't mind."

Wes liked her bravado. "There could be trouble."

"No harm in my seein' you to the edge of my grandpa's land."

The prisoners were sullen as they moved their horses eastward along the river. Cindy rode at Wes's side, keeping her rifle across her lap. She glanced at him casually as rain ran off their hat brims and down her slicker and off his leather coat. The prisoners were too far ahead to hear as she spoke.

"You must have caught them doin' somethin'."

Wes nodded, pulling his hat down tighter. He told her what had happened and what he had heard at the campfire. "Seems like they think there's a gold mine up there."

"On your land?"

Her words sounded good. His land.

"You know, Wes, if you take these men to town, there isn't anyone who's going to help you."

Wes made a face. "Perryman pinned his badge on me so I could bring 'em in, but I sure don't hanker to keep it. I still work for Hollis."

"And Hollis will be trying to break them out to hang 'em, don't you know that?"

He drew his coat up around his chin. "No, I don't. He'll be cooled off by then."

"He lost one son, and now he's nearly lost another. And he's lost some good men. He should be plenty mad. And he's probably at the end of his patience."

As they neared the Taylor ranch house, they could see the ruins of the hay barn. Horses huddled in the shed by the corral. There was a light burning in the ranch house.

"You could use some coffee," Cindy said.

"Can't stop. You go ahead."

"I said I'd ride you off the place, soon as I tell Grandpa. No telling when the other Grubers will come. You could use another rifle."

"Grubers aren't wolves. They'll be armed. I don't reckon you could kill a man."

Cindy frowned at him and spun around to ride to the ranch house. In short order, she had returned at a lope, catching up with him and reining up beside him.

"Scotty says hello," she told him. "I kept him locked up from the rain."

As daylight spread across the land in the heavy rain, they rode beyond the ranch and headed ever eastward. Soon they were at the edge of what was considered the Taylor spread.

Wes reined up. "Thanks, but you'd better go back."

"I'm going with you."

"Don't you ever do what you're told? Your folks will be worried."

"I told 'em I'm riding in with you and I'll be stayin' the night in town, so I could get supplies."

"You tell 'em about the Grubers?"

"Of course not."

He glared at her, knowing she was too stubborn to listen to reason. He continued riding in silence, and she kept pace, her black horse tossing its head.

Now and then, Sloan looked over his shoulder. Seth rode hunched up in the saddle. It was exceptionally cold, and the wind was rising, throwing the rain at them like heavy hail. The river was over its banks in places.

By noon the town was in sight. There was no one out in the rain. Two saddle horses were hunched up, heads down, at the rail in front of a saloon. A wagon without a team was in front of the general store. Otherwise, the street was empty.

Wes headed the two prisoners toward the jail. Cindy stayed in the saddle, rifle ready, as he dismounted and dragged the Grubers down. He shoved them onto the boardwalk and kicked open the door of the jail, then forced them inside.

Cindy dismounted and followed. She lit a lamp in the dark jailhouse as Wes herded the Grubers into the first cell. He checked their boots and pockets for knives. Then he untied Seth and went back out of the cell, slamming it locked. Seth rubbed his hands and then went to untie the fierce-eyed Sloan.

"You won't get away with this, Carson," Sloan warned. "My pa expected us back by noon. If we don't show, he's goin' lookin', and pretty soon he'll be ridin' in."

Wes turned his back and walked away.

The town was still silent and locked up when Wes returned from taking care of the horses. He reentered the jail to find Cindy without her slicker. She was wearing a blue jacket and riding skirt, and she was seated in the lawman's chair with her boots up on the desk and her rifle across her lap. Her long hair was spread over her shoulders, and she looked cute as a speckled fawn.

"You have to get a room at the hotel," Wes said.

"But you have to find the sheriff, see if he's all right. Go ahead. I'll watch these critters."

Wes looked at the cell where the weary Grubers had stretched out on their bunks, both snoring. "I'll see if Churchill can get someone else to pin this badge on."

"Haven't you learned anything about Shotgun Wells? You rode in and saw how the Grubers were manhandling me, and no one lifted a finger. The whole town is scared of them. Now you got two in jail, and their pa's got an army to come after them. Just who do you think is going to help you?''

Wes swallowed hard, considering her words. He was damp, tired, and cold. He needed sleep and a hot meal. Yet he could only stare at this wisp of a woman who looked cool and rested, as if she had just had eight hours sleep and a hot breakfast.

''All right,'' he said. ''I'll go to the doc's and see if Perryman's able to get over here. You watch yourself.''

''You worried about me?''

He managed a grin. ''I've given up on that.''

She smiled. ''Go ahead. I'll try to make some coffee.''

He left the jail and walked down the street in the pouring rain, over to the doctor's office. He climbed the stairs wearily and pounded on the door. Soon it opened and the squat little man peered over his spectacles.

''How's Perryman?'' Wes asked.

''He's fifty-fifty. Ain't sure. But you can talk to him.''

Inside, Wes removed his dripping hat and opened his wet leather coat for air. He saw Haney sitting in a chair, a crutch over his knee. The foreman sure looked glad to see him.

Wes walked over to the bed where the sheriff was flat on his back and heavily bandaged.

"Carson," the lawman whispered, gazing up at him, "did you get 'em?"

"They're both in jail," Wes said, sitting on a chair next to the bed. "They killed Hollis's men all right, includin' the first one. And I overheard some mighty interestin' talk. Seems Simon and Sloan killed that old prospector up in Turkey Creek. And they're wanted for robbin' an Army payroll, probably down in Texas where they come from."

The sheriff's face was pale, and he had difficulty getting his words past his lips. "Listen to me, Carson. You gotta hold 'em."

"I still work for Hollis, you know."

"No matter. You gotta do it right. I sent for the U.S. Marshal, 'counta I know he was over in Butte. Maybe two days, that's all you gotta wait."

"Then Churchill had better get me some help."

"In this town?"

"Maybe Hollis, then. He has plenty of reason. When you had your fight with the Grubers, they had already killed three of Hollis's men and wounded Reggie."

The lawman was doubtful. "The way it's rainin', them creeks will be pourin' into that river. No way Hollis can get across. That's why Haney's still here."

Wes studied this man who urgently wanted justice done. He was sorry he had gained the wrong impression when he had first come to town, but he didn't know how to apologize.

Perryman tried to talk some more, but he started coughing. The doctor shooed Wes away, but not before Wes made the lawman promise to have food sent over to the jail. He also asked him to get Churchill.

Haney hobbled after Wes, following him to the doorway. "Listen, I can get across the river. There's a way I know, down at the bend. I'll get Hollis and some men over."

"You'll get drowned," Wes protested.

"Got me a good swimmin' horse, so don't you worry."

"Anything happens to you, I'll be answerin' to Cindy's ma."

Haney grinned and shivered in the cold, wet wind, then closed the door behind Wes.

As he went down the stairs in the driving rain, Wes realized how trapped he was. Even if Haney could get across the river, Hollis would never get here in time. Wes couldn't let the Grubers go, and pretty soon, he'd be facing pandemonium with no help.

Except for Cindy.

He returned to the jail and entered, dripping wet and cold. Cindy was standing by the iron stove. There was a steaming pot of coffee and a huge kettle.

"I've got a bath going for you," she said. "In

the back room. The sheriff has three huge barrels of water in there, and I figure to put them to good use.''

''What?''

''I said you're dirty. You smell rotten.''

Wes growled under his breath, but he knew she was aware of how tired he was. She was smiling as she picked up the kettle and carried it into the small room to the right of the cells. He wondered if she ever got tired.

The Grubers were still snoring, and he figured he'd better end up just as rested as they were. He told Cindy about Haney's promise to bring help. He followed her as he talked.

The back room was apparently where the sheriff lived. There was a bunk, books on a shelf, and a lot of clothes hanging on hooks. A saddle was in the corner and bridles hung on the pegs, along with lariats and a couple of hats. There was no window. On a shelf were about two dozen empty bottles several inches in diameter with red lids, probably saved for target practice.

In the center of the wooden floor was a large iron washtub, steaming with hot water. A towel and soap were on the chair nearby. Cindy looked very proud of herself as she poured the contents of the kettle into the tub, bringing it up to half full.

Wes pulled off his coat. He was almost asleep on his feet. Cindy walked to the door, then turned with a smile.

"Get some sleep, Wes. I'll let you know if the Grubers come to town."

"What about you?"

She picked up her Winchester from where it leaned against the desk. Suddenly, there was a pounding at the door. Wes came alive and hung up his coat. He walked past Cindy, back to the front room. The Grubers continued to snore. Wes pulled his six-gun and peered out the window to the right of the door. Then he opened it to let Churchill come waddling inside.

The heavy man was sweating in his slicker. He glanced toward the cells and kept his voice in a mumble. "Doc just told me about this. Are you crazy?"

"They killed three men and wounded the sheriff and Reggie Hollis. What do you expect me to do?"

"Blast you, Carson, you gotta let 'em out. If the rest of the Grubers come to town, we'll all be killed."

Cindy drew herself up. "Why don't you just go home and lock your door, Mr. Churchill?"

Wes sat on the edge of the desk. "Better yet, send me some deputies."

Churchill wiped his brow. "No one's gonna help you, Carson. This whole town is terrified of the Grubers. Besides, you got no legal authority to lock 'em up."

"The sheriff deputized me."

Now the fat man was really upset. "Well, un-deputize yourself. Get out of here, Carson."

"When the U.S. Marshal gets here, I will."

"You're a fool. If you get killed over this, not one man in town is going to care, and not one woman is going to shed a tear for you, unless it's this crazy young woman."

Cindy leveled her Winchester repeater, aiming directly at Churchill's big belly. He stared at her, stuttered a little, then stormed out the door, barely a fit.

As the big man hurried into the rain, a scared-looking little man from the café entered, deposited four trays of food, and quickly departed.

Wes bolted and barred the door. He turned to watch Cindy as she set her rifle aside and shoved the prisoners' trays under the cell door. Then she sat with Wes as he wolfed down some food while she barely touched hers. She looked pale, the freckles on her face more visible.

"Wes, you haven't slept for twenty-four hours. You're going to need some sleep before this is over. Take your bath and sleep, please. I'll holler if there's any sign of the Grubers."

"All right, but stay away from the cell, no matter what. And when the Grubers come, you're leavin'."

He stood up slowly, aching for the bath and that hard bunk in the other room. But he paused to look down at her as she sat huddled close to the stove.

Her hair was glistening like fire in the lamplight. Rain was beating on the roof, the wind rattling the windows. He was glad she was here.

"Thanks," he said.

He gazed at her smile for a long moment, and then he headed for the back room, grateful for some rest.

In a short while, the town would explode.

## Chapter Eight

After a hot bath and some deep sleep, Wes awakened in the back room of the jailhouse. He was stiff and sore. The lamp was burning low, and he realized it was night. The rain was still heavy on the roof, and the wind was howling.

He sat up with a start, remembering where he was. He was dressed except for his boots, which he pulled on quickly. He walked around the washtub as he buckled on his six-gun and picked up his Winchester.

Hatless, he jerked open the door and hurried into the front room, where he paused. Cindy was at the desk, her boots up as she slept in the big wooden chair. Her rifle was across her lap under her right hand, but her left hand dangled at her side. With her head tilted back and her hair spilling around her, she was a wonderful sight.

He turned to look at the cell. The Grubers were sitting there watching him. Their two trays had been emptied of food and shoved back under the cell door. Sloan slowly got to his feet and walked over to the bars, gripping them angrily.

"Listen to me, Carson. Ain't no one in this town got enough guts to help you. And pretty soon our pa's gonna figure out somethin' happened to us. When he gets here, you're dead."

Cindy stirred in her chair and sat up, dropping her boots to the floor and blinking at Wes. At that moment, there was a pounding at the door.

"You see?" Sloan said, sneering triumphantly.

Wes turned down the lamp on the desk, then moved to the window to the left of the door and slid the shutter aside, but saw nothing. It was pitch-dark out there. Again, someone pounded on the door.

"Hey, open up. It's Becker."

Cindy straightened in her chair. "He's the blacksmith."

"What do you want?" Wes called.

"I got some grub for you."

Wes unbarred the door and the burly man entered, carrying sacks of food, including pots and pans.

"Couldn't get cooked grub for you," Becker said, "but I figured you was gonna be in here awhile, so I brought you plenty of supplies. Lots of coffee too."

"Becker," Sloan said with a snarl, "I ain't for-gettin' this."

"I could use a deputy," Wes said.

Becker shrugged. "Sorry, but I got a wife and newborn baby. I can't take chances."

When the man left, Wes barred the door again. Then he moved the sacks onto the table against the front wall. Sloan began to bang the cell bars.

"Hey, we're hungry, Carson. Have that pretty girl fix us some grub."

Wes scowled at him, but Cindy set about going through the sacks. She was about to empty the last sack when she paused, startled and frightened, setting it back on the table and beckoning to Wes.

He came over and looked inside. There was a small keg of gunpowder and two sticks of dynamite. He swallowed, knowing he had little experience with the explosive, yet realizing it might be just what they needed to survive. Carefully, he took the keg and sweating sticks out of the sack, setting them on the table.

He turned to Cindy. "About time you headed for the hotel. I don't want you gettin' hurt."

"I'm good with a rifle, and you got nobody else. Besides, they may not come tonight, and you'll need more sleep. You had only a few hours."

He glowered at her, but he was helpless. Short of picking her up bodily and throwing her outside, he was stuck with her for now. Yet he sure was enjoying her company while things were quiet. She was uncommonly beautiful.

"All right, but when they come, you leave."

She smiled. "We'll talk about it then."

"You're a crazy woman."

"Listen, if we were on the ranch and the Sioux or Cheyenne were cutting down on us, you'd think nothin' of me pullin' a rifle. What's the difference now?"

"The difference is it ain't necessary here."

"Isn't it?"

"There's no arguing with you, is there?"

"So why don't you give up?"

Frustrated, Wes turned to pour himself some coffee. She was the most difficult woman he had ever met, and he just didn't understand her. Yet he sure did admire her courage and persistence.

"Besides," she added, "I got my own fight with the Grubers. But right now, we'd better hope Mr. Haney got across the river and is bringing help."

"Stop your barkin' and gabbin' and fix us some grub," Sloan called out. "You got no help comin'. Everybody's afraid of us. Includin' Hollis."

Cindy prepared a supper of beans and hard biscuits. It was still raining, and the night was black, with no sign of life.

Wes pulled out the checker table and he and Cindy bent over it beside the iron stove. The rain was heavy, the wind shaking the walls and roof. Enjoying their coffee and taking turns winning, they smiled at each other often. The Grubers, their bellies full, stretched out and soon were snoring. Wes won another game, Cindy laughed, then bested him at the next.

"You're a strange woman," he said. "You don't act like other women."

"And you're a strange man. How many men are there who would be foolish enough to sit here and wait for an army to ride into town? You know Hollis may not be able to cross the river, even if he was inclined to be on your side. No one in town is going to help you. Why are you doing this?"

Wes shrugged, leaning back and sipping his coffee. "I reckon so you'll ask fool questions."

"Like what are you going to do with that dynamite?"

He straightened, his thoughts spinning. "I don't know about that dynamite. When it's that wet, it's too dangerous to move. You can't even breathe on it. But we could do somethin' with the gunpowder."

"What are you thinking?"

"The bottles the sheriff's been savin'—we can load 'em with gunpowder and some shotgun shells. Somethin' oughta explode if you hit 'em with a bullet. We'll hide 'em out in the street. They'd be easy targets if we can see 'em come mornin'. And they won't kill nobody, just scare 'em."

She hurried to the sheriff's room and brought out

an armful of the small bottles. They sat together at the table, inserting shotgun shells, then spooning the powder in carefully. They put the shells in various positions to take a bullet in place of a firing pin, hoping the whole foolish scheme would work.

"Will the rain get in?" she asked.

"Say your prayers and hope not."

"What if a horse kicks one?"

"I figure it'll take a bullet to set 'em off."

Wes pulled on his hat and slicker, then slipped out into the dark rain. He chose spots he could easily see from the jail window, such as the center of the street, making a wide half circle facing the jail about thirty feet away, with just the red lids and only part of the bottles showing.

As an afterthought, he put one under the watering trough in front of the stage and express office, which was next door to the jail and to the north side. Glancing around, he was convinced no one had seen him. They were all inside, keeping out of the cold rain.

Back in the jail, he barred the door. He had five bottles left, and he set them on the table.

Cindy had been watching out the window. Now she turned and said, "You'd better get some sleep."

He stood up and stretched. "There's a bunk in the corner behind the desk. I'll use it and sleep out here. You can have the sheriff's room."

She didn't argue. She gathered her things, then

headed for the back room and closed the door. He guessed she was asleep before she hit the bunk.

He stood a moment, surveying the front room. The only windows were the two, both shuttered under the curtains, on either side of the front door, along with a tiny one high in the first of the two cells, the one where the Grubers slept. To the right of the cells was the room where Cindy was sleeping, which had another tiny window. There was no back door. Rifle slots were in the side walls.

Between the cells and the front wall was the iron stove. Next to the front wall were the table and chairs. The desk was over between the entrance to the back room and the far wall where the extra bunk rested.

Wes made sure the front door was barred securely. He stretched out on the bunk, his six-gun across his middle, tight in his grasp, his hat over his face.

He slept well, yet was tense and ready to spring to life at any strange sound, an ability that had kept him alive while scouting Apaches.

The first strange sound came just before dawn. It was the rattle of the coffeepot on the iron stove. The Grubers were still snoring. Wes pushed his hat away from his face and looked at Cindy as she carefully measured the coffee.

"Don't forget one for the pot," he said.

She turned and smiled, her hand on her hip. "Well, there you are. You sure can snore."

He sat up, pulling his hat on. "I don't snore."

"Sure could have fooled me. Another thing. Why do cowboys always wear their hats inside? It ain't rainin' in here."

Embarrassed, he took his hat off and smoothed his hair. "Yes, ma'am."

"The rain hasn't stopped. I don't figure that Silas Gruber is out looking for his sons. He'll think they're holed up because of the storm."

"You could be right."

"That means the marshal or even Hollis could get here before the Grubers."

"How long will it take for the river to go back down if it stops raining?"

She was thoughtful. "I'm not sure. I think a day, maybe more."

He stretched lazily. "You look fresh as a daisy."

"That's what Cliff used to say."

"Cliff?"

"That Cliff Sellers. He called on me a few times. Then for some reason, he disappeared. I thought maybe the trouble with the Grubers scared him off. Next thing I knew, he was fixin' to marry Angela Hollis and her father's ranch."

"That bother you?"

She nodded. "A little bit."

Wes felt a flash of jealousy, but he wasn't sure if it was over her or Angela. Things were getting plenty mixed up.

Five years ago, Angela had been a devastating experience, lingering like an ache in his gut. Cindy was a western breeze, rising cool from the land, her hair as dark red as the wide horizon on a Texas morning.

Cindy set about fixing breakfast. The prisoners awakened to the sounds of pots and pans. Rain continued to pound the roof, but the wind had subsided.

Abruptly, they heard the heavy roll of loud thunder, the walls shaking and the roof rattling. Then another roll of thunder so loud, Cindy looked frightened.

"Listen to that," Sloan called. "It's clearing up, Carson. My pa will be here before the Hollis bunch can ever get across the river. You better be sayin' your prayers."

Silas Gruber was scratching himself and sitting at the table in his ranch house. Rain and wind beat at the structure, and he was enjoying the hot fire in the hearth.

Martha Gruber was serving breakfast and fussing about the thunder. "Maybe we ought to head for California," she suggested.

He grunted. "You ain't never satisfied."

"You never know when Texas is gonna catch up with us."

"We left no trail."

"Silas, we got an Army payroll, remember?"

"Didn't leave no witnesses."

"But the Army ain't gonna forget about the money."

"They'll never figure it was us, so just stop your naggin'."

Just then Simon came out of his room, no shirt over his long underwear, suspenders holding up his britches, his six-gun strapped to his hip. He yawned and stretched.

"Pa, it seems to me that Seth and Sloan shoulda been back by now."

"They musta holed up in the storm," Martha said.

"They ain't much for bein' out in bad weather," Simon insisted. "Somethin' must have gone wrong."

"Then you go look for 'em," his father said.

Simon snorted. "I ain't that worried."

"Maybe they couldn't get back across the river," Martha said. "It must have been raining before they could get out of Turkey Creek."

There was a pounding at the door. Simon got up to open it and allow the man inside. It was Miller, out of breath, his slicker and hat dripping rain.

"Miller," Silas said, "you got a can tied to your tail or somethin'?"

The cowhand sank down on the bench by the door, exhausted. "I near killed my horse gettin' here from town. Mr. Gruber, I got bad news for you. Your two boys, Sloan and Seth, they're in jail for killin' some of Hollis's men and for shootin' his son and the sheriff.''

Silas nearly choked on his bread. ''What?''

''Your sons, they're in jail.''

Martha was furious. ''They got proof?''

Miller shrugged. ''Well, the sheriff's still alive, though just barely, and so's Reggie Hollis. They can get your sons hanged.''

Silas slammed his fist down on the table, rattling the dishes. ''Them fool kids! I told 'em to leave no witnesses.''

Miller dried his face with his bandanna. ''Anyhow, they're in jail, waitin' for the U.S. Marshal.''

''Yeah? Who's got 'em locked up?''

''That there Wes Carson. He's a deputy now.''

Silas grimaced, his fists clenched tight. ''I knowed he was trouble. Hollis put him up to it, you can bet on it.''

''There's one good thing,'' Miller said. ''Ain't no way Hollis can get across the river to come and help Carson, not as long as it's rainin'.''

''But it's gonna clear up,'' Simon said.

''We got to get to town now.'' Silas got to his feet. ''Miller, you get Maddox and some of the boys. We're goin' in and teachin' that fool Carson a lesson afore Hollis can butt in.''

''How many men has Carson got with him?'' Simon asked.

Miller grinned. ''No one will help him. Except

that girl, Cindy Taylor. She's in the jail with him. And I got to tell you, she's a crack shot."

Silas was amused but still grim. "All right, then. Let's go."

Martha leaned back in her chair, looking weary. "It seems like folks just won't leave the Grubers alone."

"Don't you worry," Silas told her. "We'll take care of this in short order. Your boys will be home for supper."

Reed Hollis was pacing in front of the hearth in his elegant home. His daughter, Angela, still in her dressing gown, was trying to calm him.

"Blast!" he said. "Here I tried to get Reggie to the doctor and the blamed river turned us back. I shoulda gone and crossed over with Carson before the flooding."

"That would have been the long way around," Angela pointed out gently. "Besides, Reggie wasn't hurt that bad. You said yourself that the bullet went clean through his ear and just grazed his head. He ate a huge meal last night, and he's upstairs snoring away."

Hollis sighed. "I guess you're right."

"You know Reggie always makes a big thing out of being hurt. Remember whenever he was bucked off, he couldn't walk for a week? And a few months ago, he hurt his back, or so he said, and we had to wait on him hand and foot. He just needs attention and sympathy. You know you always did like Randy best, and Reggie could tell.''

''Well, right now, I'm worried about Carson.''

''Yes, and I worried about him at Fort Apache—for about two days. Then I realized that he was indestructible. He would voluntarily go out to the most terrible fights, but he always came back. Other men died all around him, but he just kept riding out.''

''But this time, he's in real trouble. If he ain't dead, then he got them Gruber boys and took 'em to town, which means the Grubers will be after him. And the Grubers could have killed Randy. That's why you sent for Wes, remember?''

''Yes, I remember. And I'm glad the river's flooded. Let him handle it. That's why you pay him, isn't it?''

''What if it was Cliff?''

''Oh, Father, Cliff would never get mixed up in that kind of trouble. He's an educated gentleman.''

''Yeah, well, bein' a gentleman don't keep you alive out here.''

Angela smiled. ''You're just envious of his good manners. When we're married, I'll be going back East with him. His family is high society, you know.''

''What about Carson? You were sure fussin' about

him down in Fort Apache. You wanted to marry *him*.''

"Only because I knew you wouldn't let me."

"That's what you say now."

She smiled. "You're right. I guess I never really stopped loving him, but I don't like a man I can't control."

"So you're gonna marry Sellers?"

"Of course."

Hollis frowned. "As soon as the river drops, I'm takin' some of the boys to town to see what's happening."

"And I'll go with you. I'm to be fitted for my wedding dress."

"Men could be killin' each other, and you're worried about your dress?"

"Father, if women took time to worry about all the foolishness that men get themselves into, we would never have time to be women."

"Now, that don't make sense."

Just then, there was a knock at the door, followed by more-insistent pounding. Hollis walked over and opened it in time to catch a staggering Haney. The cowhand was barely able to stand as the rancher helped him over to the hearth.

When Haney spilled out his tale of Shotgun Wells, Hollis was astounded. "So you mean to tell me Wes has them two in jail and nobody is helpin' him?"

"Just that girl, Cindy Taylor."

Angela's face darkened. "Why is she there?"

"She can handle a rifle," Haney said.

"You rest up," Hollis told Haney. "I'll get some of the men. Is the river down?"

"I crossed at the bend, down by the cottonwoods, but it's mighty tricky. Any man what tries it had better be on a swimmin' horse. Unless the water drops, that is."

"Maybe we can beat the Grubers in."

Haney wiped his face with his bandanna. "I don't know, but I'm goin' with you."

Angela was distressed. "Father, you can't go. Silas Gruber would like nothing better than to have an excuse to shoot you down."

"I'm goin' too," Reggie said from the stairs.

"You ain't well, son."

"You listen to me, Pa. I'm tougher than you think and tougher than Randy ever was, and I'm ridin' with you."

Angela drew herself up. "Then I'd better go and keep you both out of trouble."

Hollis spun on his heel and charged out into the early light of day.

While Hollis was gathering his men, Wes was enjoying a good breakfast prepared by Cindy. He liked the way she hummed to herself now and then. When he had fallen for Angela, he had not thought much beyond her pretty face. But now, watching

Cindy, he wondered how it really would be, to have a ranch, a home, with a woman like this seeing to his needs, working cattle with him, hunting at his side, and giving him sass to no end.

He grinned at his thoughts, and she kept humming.

Later in the day, Cindy served bread and jam with more coffee. Wes only had to look at her smile, her long red hair, and the freckles on her nose, to realize a man could love two women in his lifetime, if he allowed it to happen.

The Grubers were lounging in their cell, growling and complaining, yet promising Wes's imminent death.

"Any minute now," Sloan called.

Wes ignored them, but he could feel a twinge of anxiety. All he had to help him now was a woman, and he couldn't allow that. As soon as the Grubers came, she was leaving.

There was a knock at the door after Cindy went into the back room. Wes draped cloth over the dynamite sticks. He peered out the window. It was Churchill, his fat face dripping with more than the drizzling rain. With him was a big sandy-haired dude whose blue eyes gazed around the jail as Wes allowed them inside.

Churchill was worried. "Listen to me, Carson. The storm is clearing up. You don't have any help.

You got to let 'em go, or this town will be torn apart.''

Wes held his temper. ''You just keep both sides of the street clear for a hundred feet in every direction. Don't want no folks hurt.''

Churchill wiped his brow. ''Listen, Carson, I brought Cliff Sellers here. He's about to marry Angela Hollis, and he can tell you this is not what Hollis wants.''

''How so?'' Wes asked, looking the dude over. The man sure was pretty and neat and clean. So this was what Angela wanted, after all. It hurt more than he had expected. He told himself it was just his pride.

Sellers smiled pleasantly. ''I don't think Mr. Hollis wants the town torn apart. He'd probably tell you to let them go on their own recognizance.''

''Just do as I say,'' Wes insisted, ''and clear the street.''

''What you got in mind?'' the fat man demanded.

''Just do as I say.''

''I've been trying to help you, boys,'' Churchill called to the prisoners. ''You be sure and tell your father.''

When the fat man and the dude left, the Grubers had a good laugh.

Wes sat down and thought about Sellers. So that was the man Angela chose to marry. A rosy-cheeked Easterner who had also courted Cindy. There was no way Wes was going to like the man.

Cindy came out of the back room. "I heard all that. You ought to realize by now you're not getting help from any of them."

"Look, the Grubers could be here at any time. You get out of here now."

"I could get up on the top of the general store and hit some of the bottles."

"And be a target yourself? Not a chance."

"That's exactly what I'm going to do, and you can't stop me. There's a false front up there, and they won't even know where the shot came from."

"Nothin' doin'. You get out of here and head for home."

"I'm going to borrow your leather coat and take some of those extra shells."

Wes stood up and faced her. "I said no. I don't need help, least of all from a woman."

She drew herself up. "You can't do this all by yourself. When are you going to get that through your hard head?"

He glared down at her. She smiled up at him.

Exasperated, he stood watching her as she walked over to his coat and pulled it on. She stuffed the pockets with extra shells and picked up her Winchester.

She turned with a smile. "Don't worry. I'll be careful."

"I'm warning you. Don't you do nothin'. Sit up

there if you insist, but don't you be shootin' anything. I can get a good shot from here."

"There's a ladder up behind the store. I'd better get over there and out of sight. The sun's out now, so I'll be warm enough. Looks like the rain is done for."

She moved to the doorway, but turned to look up at him. Her eyes were glistening, her lips parted, and she poked at his belly with the butt of her rifle. "Don't do anything foolish, you hear?"

"Will you get out of here?"

She smiled and opened the door.

Outside, Cindy waded across the deep mud. Some of the bottles had almost disappeared, but she was too smart to stop and adjust their positions, not wanting to call attention to their existence. She moved to the far boardwalk and the general store, which was closed, continuing through the alley to the ladder that was attached to the back of the building.

She had difficulty climbing while holding on to her Winchester, but she made it to the roof. There she saw planks and oil paper with some rocks and buckets on it, probably holding back the rain from leaks. She moved to the false front where she saw cracks in the boards, just right for a good shot at the street. It was cold and damp, but the sun was warm.

She turned a bucket over and sat down, gazing through a crack toward the street. She was thinking of Wes Carson, for he was like no man she had ever met. He was a wild one, all right, but she could throw a pretty good noose, so he had better watch out. She smiled at the thought.

Back at the jail, Wes was seated at the table with more of the thick, heavy coffee.

Seth, who had been silent all this time, sat up on his bunk. "Listen, Carson, we oughta be able to make a deal."

"I have a deal with Hollis, for Turkey Creek."

Sloan gripped the bars. "That's a promise Hollis ain't ever gonna keep."

"Don't you worry about it. Right now, you're in here for murder. I figure you boys even killed Randy Hollis."

Sloan shook his head. "You'd better look closer to home for that."

"Look, Carson," Seth said as he stood up and gripped the bars. "All you want is money, right? My pa will pay plenty to let us out. And nobody in this town would stop you."

Wes stood up and picked up one of the sweating sticks of dynamite from the table. "See this stuff? When it looks like that, it can explode at the drop of a hat."

Color fading, Sloan backed away and sat on his bunk.

Wes carefully put the dynamite back on the table.

Then he walked to the window and peered outside, just in time to see twenty horsemen coming in from the south side of town, crowded together and gathering in front of the jail, some of the horses kicking mud over the bottles as they came forward. All wore slickers, and their hats were pulled down tight.

The old man in front had to be Silas Gruber. The young man on his left had to be Simon, who looked just like his brothers, all with hawklike faces and dark mustaches. Silas had a beard.

On Silas's right was Chuck Maddox, his buglike eyes bulging, his concho-dotted hatband gleaming in the sunlight.

He recognized Miller and Swanson from when he had shot the Brazos Kid. The others looked more like gunmen than cowhands.

Every one of them looked mean as sin.

# Chapter Nine

As he watched the Grubers and their men gather in the street, Wes noticed that there was no sign of Rio. He figured the man was on his way to Alaska, maybe looking for wife number five. He grinned at the thought.

But he sobered as he realized the horsemen were too close and he couldn't see any of the bottles. They had ridden right up to the hitching rails.

"Sheriff!" Silas yelled. "I wanta see my sons."

"Come back tomorrow," Wes shouted through the window.

Silas drew his six-gun and started firing as Wes shoved the shutter in place. Instantly, the other men started rapid fire at the jail. Bullets thudded at the walls and some cut through, hitting the table and stove. The roar was like thunder.

The prisoners dived for the floor. Wes knelt low on the opposite side of the door, staring at the dynamite on the table as it rolled about, miraculously unaffected. Wes realized sweat was drenching his clothes.

"Had enough?" Silas shouted.

There was a long moment of silence. Carefully, Wes rose to peer through the shutter. He couldn't get a good shot at the bottles without exposing himself. Across the street, he could see the false front above the general store, but there was no sign of Cindy.

"You near killed one of your sons," Wes called.

"You're lyin'!" Silas barked. "Now come on out afore we break down that wall."

"There's dynamite in here. You came within an inch."

Again there was a long silence. The gunmen looked plenty mean as they sat on their restless, snorting horses. Wes knew they could fire off another barrage without hesitation. He also knew they could break down the door.

Suddenly, a rifle fired from the false front over the general store. The bullet hit the bottle behind Silas. The explosion was deafening and sent mud and water flying.

Silas's mount reared and bucked and whinnied while he held to the horn. The other horses bucked and spun around. Three men were thrown down in the mud. Maddox clung to his saddle and managed to stay seated. Simon was half out of the saddle but recovered. The horses danced frantically in the mud.

"What the blazes was that?" Simon demanded.

Again the rifle cracked. The watering trough in front of the express office exploded. Water rained down, boards flying. Again the horses bucked and spun around, crashing into each other. This time Silas was thrown over backward, his horse going with him and nearly falling on him as he rolled aside.

Simon clung to the horn as his horse jumped around.

Silas got to his feet, covered with mud and cursing. He looked up at the top of the general store, but he could see nothing. He looked around. There was no sign of anyone in town.

"Blast you, Carson!" he shouted.

Wes leaned near the window, watching the angry gunmen. He felt a sigh of relief as they began to lead their horses up the street toward the livery. He still couldn't see Cindy, but he knew her temptation would be great as the Gruber men passed that bottle on the far edge of the circle.

When the bottle was behind them, the rifle cracked once more. The explosion sent the horses into wild disarray. The men on foot frantically fought to hold the reins. Two riders were dumped in the mud, their horses running wild down the street. The other horses bucked and kicked while the men held on to saddle horns and manes.

Wes grinned to himself, but he saw Silas looking again at the top of the general store. Suddenly, Silas and his son Simon were headed for it.

Wes fired, his shot hitting the boardwalk in front of them. The two men paused. Silas shook his fist at Wes, then spun and charged up the street with Simon at his heels.

Silas was furious as they entered the livery with their horses. "Who in this blasted town has the guts to stand up to a Gruber? Whoever's on that roof is gonna get it. Simon, you take one of the boys and go around back of that store and get up there. Hurry now, before that fella gets away."

Back at the jail, Wes moved the dynamite into the back room, very carefully. Then he returned to the window just in time to see two men running behind the buildings on the other side of the street, heading for the general store. His face burned hot as his gut turned cold.

Heart pounding, Wes unbarred the door. He darted outside with his Winchester just as Cindy appeared from the alley. She was running, red hair flying, but suddenly Simon was behind her. Before she could reach the center of the street, her boots bogged down. The man's big arm wrapped around her neck from behind, jerking her off her feet.

Wes paused on the boardwalk in front of the jail, his rifle cocked and ready.

Simon had his arms around Cindy's neck and waist, her arms pinned down, her back to him as her feet kicked at the air. She was gasping for breath and fighting furiously, hair whipping about her face.

Next to her was Chuck Maddox, his six-gun aimed at her head. The man was sneering. "Hold it, Carson. One step and she's dead," he warned.

"I think not," Wes said coolly, his rifle still aimed. "Silas was plannin' to trade her for Sloan and Seth, and I don't figure he's gonna cotton to you pullin' that trigger."

Maddox's eyes narrowed. He was thinking and not moving. Simon, however, was backing away with Cindy.

The sun was in Wes's eyes, so he moved to the left of the trio and into the street, forcing Simon to move away from the buildings as he struggled to hold the squirming Cindy. Wes could only pray that the other gunmen were still at the livery, as it was now behind him.

"All right, Maddox," he said. "Maybe it's time you and me had it out."

Maddox sneered with sudden delight, lowering his six-gun. His nose seemed to twitch as his lips rolled back over his yellow teeth.

"No!" Simon growled. "You come with me, Maddox. You're gettin' paid to do what we tell you."

Maddox slowly holstered his six-gun as Wes carefully moved to prop his rifle against the nearest hitching rail. He stepped farther from it, back into the street, his hand loose and resting near his holster.

Cindy was fighting furiously, but her efforts only further cut off her breath as Simon's arm tightened around her neck.

Wes faced Maddox in the warmth of the sunlight, his boots sinking in the mud. His shirt was damp, and his stomach churned. He didn't know how fast Maddox was, but far and wide the man had a reputation as a cold-blooded killer who had never been faced down in a fight.

If Wes was to die here and now, the Grubers would take Cindy and not only get the prisoners out of jail, but also use her to get Taylor off his land. There was more at stake than Wes's life, and he swallowed hard, a lump stuck in his throat.

"All right, Carson," Maddox said. "I heard a lot of fancy talk about you. Now, Brazos, he was all mouth, and so was Sal Gruber, so I ain't figurin' you to be as fast as I been hearin'."

Wes slowly lifted his left hand and shoved his hat back a little from his damp forehead. His mouth was so dry it hurt. His legs felt as if they were going to buckle. He wondered if he was going to die right here in the mud.

Maddox spoke from the corner of his mouth to Simon.

"Count to three, Simon."

"One—"

Wes was stiff but his right arm was loose. Maddox had taken a stance with his feet apart. There was no one outside to watch this show except Simon and Cindy, but Maddox was enjoying it just the same, certain half the town was peering out from behind the closed curtains up and down the street.

"Two—"

Cindy squealed and kicked some more.

"Three."

Wes and Maddox drew at the same time, fanning the hammer as they pulled the trigger, their faces hot and breath tight.

Bullets sped from the smoking barrels with loud blasts.

It seemed an eternity before the slug slammed into Wes's right arm near the shoulder, spitting blood. In that instant, he saw Maddox drop to his knees with blood on his chest, but Maddox aimed again. They both shot at the same time.

Maddox gasped and fired again as Wes fired back.

Dropping to his elbows, Maddox tried to lift his six-gun as he stared in dismay at Wes's boots. He couldn't look up and abruptly dropped his face in the mud.

Wes came forward and used his right boot to turn the man over; Maddox was dead. He turned away and clamped his left hand over his bleeding right shoulder, feeling sudden pain. Hot blood ran freely through his fingers. His right arm was now numb and tingling at the wrist.

Then he spun around to see Simon frantically trying to back away with Cindy still tight in his arms. Wes started for him, and Simon suddenly acted.

As Simon's right arm dropped from her waist to reach for his gun, Cindy fought furiously with her freed hands, clawing at his face and arms. Then she kicked him square in the knees with both boots.

He yelped and dropped her into the mud. She fell on her hands and knees and crawled away as Wes faced the man.

Simon saw Wes's six-gun aimed at his gut, and he froze.

"Ain't you gonna give me a chance?"

Wes slowly holstered his six-gun, his fury still hot over the way Simon had manhandled Cindy. Any man who mistreated a woman, horse, or dog was in plenty of trouble around Wes, but when the woman was Cindy, anger rose like boiling oil in his veins.

But Simon knew he couldn't outdraw Wes. He started backing away. "I ain't gonna pull on you, Carson."

"I'm takin' you to jail."

"What for?"

"Transportin' a woman against her will."

Simon saw the blood running down Wes's right shoulder. In that moment, he realized there was a chance that Wes's gun arm was numbed. His eyes narrowed. Then he suddenly drew his six-gun and fired. Wes drew at the same instant and shot the man between the eyes, but Simon's bullet whistled past Wes's ear.

Simon doubled up, then jerked backward like a falling scarecrow and lay on his back in the mud, eyes wild as he kicked his legs and tried to lift his six-gun. Then he slowly dropped both arms and lay still.

Wes checked to make sure he was dead, then rose and turned.

Cindy had recovered her rifle and was wiping it on her skirts. She was still shaken but had that bounce-back quality he admired. He could tell she was plenty nervous and was about to say something smart to hide her fear.

She came closer. "If I hadn't kicked Simon, he would have shot you, and you wouldn't have fired because you'd have been afraid to hit me. So I guess I saved your hide, didn't I?"

Ever amazed at her, Wes picked up his rifle with his right hand and started back toward the open jail door with Cindy on his heels. His right shoulder was hurting plenty, and his right arm was numb down to his wrist. He had already lost a lot of blood, and he was feeling dazed.

He glanced back at her. "I don't know why I bothered to come after you."

"Hey, I hit those bottles, didn't I?"

He stopped abruptly and looked down at her rosy cheeks and sparkling green eyes. She was the most beautiful woman he had ever met, and yet she was so complex. He could see mixtures of fear and courage, distress and joy, alternately coloring her face.

She moved closer, lowering her Winchester. Her voice was soft as cotton. "I like wearing your coat."

She was a constant surprise, and he was liking every minute of it. A crooked smile held his lips tight. He gazed at her with such burning warmth, he momentarily forgot the pain in his shoulder. Cindy frowned with concern.

"You'd better see the doc."

"I've got to get back inside the jail, and I got no idea what to do with you."

"I'll get the doctor to come here."

"Nothin' doin'. I ain't lettin' you out of my sight."

"So you'll let me help you?"

"You can come and fix my arm while I think about it."

At that moment, they heard a commotion up the street. Eighteen men on foot had appeared out of the livery, all out of range of a pistol, and none had rifles in their hands. They were staring. Suddenly, Silas started running down the boardwalk on the opposite side of the street.

Wes hurried into the jail, Cindy at his heels, and she slammed the door behind them. He helped her lift the bar and put it in place. Then they each pulled back a shutter on the windows on either side of the door and peered out into the sunlight.

Silas was running crazily through the deep mud to where his son lay. Red-faced and furious, the old man knelt in the mud, grabbed Simon's arm, and shook it wildly.

"Simon, you ain't dead! Get up, blast you!"

But Simon didn't move. Miller came to kneel over Maddox's body, then rose, dumbfounded. "I didn't think anybody could take Maddox," he said, his voice uneven.

Silas struggled to his feet, his big body trembling. "Carson, I'm gonna kill you!" he yelled.

It was then that a buckboard entered the street from the south. A woman sat on the wagon seat behind a team of blacks. She was small and gray, wearing a heavy cape. As she neared, she started losing all color.

Silas walked over as she pulled up the team. "Martha, Carson got Simon."

She didn't answer. With Miller's help, he lifted Simon and Maddox into the back of the wagon. Then

Miller jumped onto the flat tailgate, while Silas climbed aboard with his wife.

Silent, she drove the team up toward the livery where the other men waited. Soon they all disappeared inside.

Wes drew a deep breath, his left hand still clutching his bleeding right shoulder. He leaned on the windowsill, so dazed he could barely stand. His right arm was still numb, his fingers tingling.

Cindy straightened, setting her rifle aside. "Let's get that shoulder."

He sat near the iron stove while the Grubers watched from their jail cell. As Cindy worked to tear away his shirt and wash the torn flesh, she seemed at a loss for words. Wes, too, had nothing to say, and he endured the pain as she probed at his wound to discover the bullet had gone clean through.

Sloan was leaning on the bars. "So, he got your gun arm did he? Was it Maddox?" he asked with a sneer.

Cindy turned to look at him, her chin up. "Maddox is dead. So is Simon."

Sloan's face darkened. "What?"

Seth got to his feet and grabbed the bars, frantic. "You killed Simon?"

Cindy ignored them and began to bandage Wes's arm. "You've lost a lot of blood," she told him softly. "You'd better lie down. I'll watch."

He looked up at her with admiration. She was

soft, vulnerable, but brave as any man, and here at his side. He would never have expected Angela to be here, but Cindy, well, she was right for the job.

He got to his feet and walked slowly and carefully across the room. He stretched out on the bunk, and she came to sit at his side, putting wet towels on his brow. He gazed up at her, then looked toward the door.

"Don't worry," she said. "I'll wake you if they come."

"My arm," he whispered. "It's numb."

"Keep it raised." Gently, she took his right hand and laid it on his chest. His fingers closed over hers, then slid aside as he let himself fall asleep.

Cindy hesitated, gazing down at him, then rose and went back to the front windows to watch the street. She saw Churchill and Sellers heading for the livery, and that made her curious.

While Cindy remained on guard, the livery barn was filled with the hot anger of the Grubers.

"First Sal," Martha was saying, "then Simon. We got to get our boys out, Silas."

He nodded, standing back as the men wrapped Simon and Maddox in blankets, then carried them away from the wagon and into the back of the livery.

It was then that Churchill and Sellers appeared in the doorway. Churchill's fear of the Grubers was barely hidden in the fat folds of his face.

"Mr. Gruber, can we have a word with you?"

Silas tugged at his beard and walked toward them. The three men walked out into the sunlight. Silas was fighting to control his grief, letting his anger settle hot in his gut.

"Mr. Gruber," Churchill began, "we understand how you feel. Now this is Mr. Sellers, and he's going to marry Angela Hollis, so you can see, he can help settle things down."

"I don't see that at all," Silas said. "If you want to keep this town in one piece, you get my boys out of jail and let me hang Wes Carson, here and now."

Sweat was forming on Churchill's brow. "Nobody's helping Carson, you can see that. But he'd shoot us down if we went near the jail now."

"So what do you want, if you ain't gonna do nothin'?"

"Well, the U.S. Marshal's on his way. If you could just wait—"

A shot rang out, singing through Churchill's hat, and it went flying. The fat man turned white, his lips quivering.

They turned to see Martha Gruber standing in the doorway with a rifle still aimed at Churchill.

"We ain't waitin'," she said. "Now get."

Sellers swallowed hard. "Now, Mrs. Gruber, we want to help."

"What for?" she demanded.

"For one thing," Sellers said, lowering his voice,

"Angela Hollis is still in love with Wes Carson, and I have to do something about that."

Martha slowly let the rifle drop to her side. "All right, that makes sense. But what you got in mind?"

Churchill spoke up. "Sooner or later, he has to let the girl out of the jail. She wouldn't be there if she wasn't sweet on him. You could, uh, use her for a trade for your sons."

"What about you, Churchill?" Silas growled. "What's in for it for you?"

The fat man smiled. "I always wanted to be a judge. If you was runnin' this town, you could make it happen."

Silas chortled. "Sounds interestin'."

"And don't forget," Sellers said, "that Carson's going to need some sleep. Maybe an hour before daylight, while they're still sleeping, you could take some poles and break down the door. It's only a couple of inches thick, and the hinges are rusty."

"And if he's waitin' for us?"

"You got plenty of men," Churchill reminded him.

Silas rubbed his beard. "Might be better that way. It would give us time to bury our boy."

Martha nodded sadly and turned back into the livery.

Silas looked up and down the street. All the shades were drawn. Shutters were closed. Not a creature ventured outside anywhere, not so much as a puppy dog.

"On the other hand," Silas said, "you might be stallin' until Hollis can get here."

"Maybe," Sellers replied, "but you could be waiting for him. Get set up on the roofs."

Silas grunted. "For a future son-in-law, you don't care much what happens to him. Unless you're thinkin' if he's dead, you get the ranch when you marry Angela."

"That's just what I was thinking."

Silas turned back into the livery, sliding the big door closed behind him.

Churchill looked north toward the hills, beyond which lay the river. "You think he's coming?" he asked.

"He'll come." Sellers smiled and turned away, the big man on his heels.


Back at the jail, Wes was sleeping soundly while Cindy kept her post at the windows. It was late afternoon. She made fresh coffee and began to prepare supper.

"Hey," Sloan called, "why don't you come over here and bring us some coffee?"

"Later," she said. "When Wes wakes up."

"He sure looks like his right arm is done for."

"Don't you worry about it."

"Hey, honey, I ain't worried. I'm just curious."

She heated up beans and seared some bacon in a frying pan on the iron stove. Then she walked over to the window and looked out again. The sun was low, casting long shadows in the street. She and Wes had better get some help soon.

And where was Hollis? She wondered if he would ever come.

Suddenly she heard noise from the north, and she cast her gaze in that direction. Riders were coming! It was Hollis, his son, and Angela in the lead. Behind them were seven men, including Haney.

Before she could turn to awaken Wes, gunfire rained down on the riders from the rooftops. Hollis's bay reared and spun. Angela's horse bucked and threw her off her sidesaddle and down into the mud, turning her green outfit brown.

The other riders were frantically trying to fire back, but they were falling left and right. Haney went down into the mud, fighting to pull his weapon.

Wes sat up so fast his head spun. He grabbed his six-gun in his left hand and hurried to the window, gazing past Cindy to see the slaughter. He felt sick to his stomach.

"Stay here," he said.

"Don't go out there," she pleaded. "You'll be exposed."

"I've got to stop it."

He grabbed a Winchester from the rack and started to unbar the door, just as the firing came to a halt.

He went back to the window and saw Hollis crawling in the mud, Angela helping him.

Sellers had run into the street, waving his arms to stop the firing, and for some reason, Gruber called off the killing. The dude then ran to Angela's side, helping her with her father. Wes could see no one on the roofs.

Hollis was standing now, blood on his left thigh. He looked at his men, all dead but Haney, who was getting up unsteadily, bleeding at the head. Reggie had blood on his shirt, but he was crawling toward his father.

Wes unbarred the door. "Don't let anyone in," he told Cindy as she barred the door behind him.

He stormed up the street to where Reed Hollis was on his knees next to Reggie, who had rolled over on his back. Sellers was standing with his arm around a frightened, muddy Angela.

Tears were running down Reed Hollis's face as he cradled his son against his good thigh. "Reggie, you're hit bad. We've got to get you to the doc."

Reggie stared up at his father. "I can't see you, Pa."

"Hang on, son. Don't try to talk."

"But, Pa, you got to know. Me and Randy, we was havin' a fight. I didn't mean it, Pa. My gun just went off."

Reed's eyes nearly closed in agony. "What are you sayin'?"

"I killed Randy, Pa. He wanted me to be like him. You wanted me to be like him. Forgive me, Pa."

Hollis took a deep breath. "Reggie, it's all right."

"Pa, I can't see you. I can't see nothin'."

"Say your prayers, son."

And Reggie, still staring blankly at his father, died in the rancher's arms. Hollis doubled up, dragging his son against him and choking on his tears, sobs racking his body.

Haney wiped his eyes. Angela broke free of Sellers and knelt to hug her father.

Churchill appeared from the alley, his face dotted with sweat. "Mr. Hollis, I don't know who done this. But we'll take care of your son and those other men. You get to the doctor."

Hollis shook his head, but Haney pulled him and his daughter to their feet. "He's right, Mr. Hollis. Come on."

Angela turned to gaze up at Wes, even as Sellers' arm tightened around her. "Oh, Wes, poor Reggie, and all those men."

"Good men," Haney muttered. "Just four didn't come. Pete and Barney and two others. They was up at the line shack."

Hollis leaned on Haney. "Angela, you go with Cliff somewhere safe."

She hesitated, still gazing at Wes, then she spoke softly. "Maybe your way is right after all, Wes."

Sellers turned her around and headed her across the street toward the nearest café.

Haney and Reed Hollis walked along with Wes. Tears still trickled down the rancher's face as Wes filled them in on what had been happening.

"As soon as we get fixed up," Hollis said, "we're comin' to help."

"Who's in the jail now?" Haney asked.

"Cindy Taylor," Wes said, "but as soon as I get some help, she's leaving."

Wes stopped in front of the jail, watching them head for the doctor's office. Cindy unbarred the door and he entered.

"What's happened?" Sloan demanded, gripping the cell bars.

Ignoring the Grubers, Wes put his Winchester on the rack. He was still weak, and he sat down in a chair near the iron stove.

"You're bleeding again," Cindy observed. She pulled back his shirt and started to remove the bandage. As she worked, he sat staring up at her. Tears were in her eyes. She had seen a lot of death in the street, and her lips were quivering.

"Hollis and Haney will be here," he told her, wincing as she tugged at the bandage. "You'll have to go with Angela and Sellers."

"What if they grab me again? I'd be a hostage. But with two more men in here, I'll be safe, honest."

"I don't want you hurt."

She avoided his gaze as she wrapped on a new bandage. "I'll heat up the food and add some more beans if we're having company. Why don't you lie down awhile?"

"No, it's gettin' dark. Things are gonna happen now."

When Hollis and Haney came to the jail and were let inside, they sat down at the table, but neither could eat. They were still sick over the death of their men and Hollis's son. They drank the hot coffee and listened to Wes.

"They'll rush us come dark. We've got to put everything we can against the door and front wall," he said.

Haney nodded. "Let's get at it."

Hobbling around, Reed picked up some of the chairs. Haney and Wes moved the desk and a cabinet against the front of the jail. They hauled out the bed from the back room, along with a chest of drawers, and shoved them in place but left access to the windows.

Haney had seen the dynamite on the shelf in the back room. "What can we do with that? It's sweatin', and it ain't safe. Just kickin' it might set it off."

Hollis shrugged. "We might need it. Let's put it out front where it'll do some good."

To the prisoners' dismay, the two dynamite sticks were put in a bucket and placed just out of their reach in front of their cells.

"What's that for?" Sloan demanded.

"To keep your pa at bay," Haney said harshly.

With the wall and door barricaded, Wes, Haney, and Hollis rested on the remaining chairs. Cindy was allowed the bunk, but she moved about, refilling their cups.

"Puttin' that stuff there won't help none," Sloan called out. "My pa's gonna come right through that door."

Hollis turned in his chair. "You shut up back there. You're both gonna hang. Your pa, too, for killin' my son and some mighty good men."

Sloan grunted. "Listen, old man, your son Reggie had a lot of hate for his brother, and I wouldn't put it past him if he didn't—"

Hollis jumped up with a roar, drawing his six-gun. Wes grabbed his arm and shoved him back down in the chair. Haney came and stood between Hollis and the cell, then pulled his chair in front of Hollis and sat down.

Haney took out his harmonica and leaned back in his chair. He began to play soft music, while the others tried to relax. It was dark outside, so Wes lit the lamp in the corner near the bunk, setting it on the floor against the wall with the light turned low. He gazed down at Cindy, who was sitting on the bunk. "It's your turn to sleep."

"No, I'm going to help. I'll just rest my eyes."

But when she lay back, she went sound asleep.

Wes stood looking down at her in wonder. And he thought of Angela, out there with Sellers. Things seemed right, somehow.

He rejoined the men and told them about Cindy's bravery, the way she had shot the bottles from the rooftop, and how she had fought her way free from Simon.

Hollis wiped his eyes and nodded. "She's different, all right."

"Try to get some sleep," Wes said. "The blankets are on the floor in the back room. Don't worry, if things happen, you'll hear it."

Haney got up and went into the back room, but Hollis hesitated. "I want to apologize to you, Wes."

"What for?"

"I always thought you were just a maverick gun."

"Maybe I am."

"What you're doin' here is the work of a man."

Wes felt his face burning. The rancher's words hit right at the heart, and he couldn't spill out his thanks. He helped the man to his feet, Hollis's hand on his shoulder.

Wes swallowed hard and stood frozen as the rancher went to the back room. He glanced at the prisoners, who had lain back sullenly on their bunks, and he wiped his brow.

Maybe he had been a maverick gun at that. Angela had been right about his wild life of violence. He sat down to have another cup of coffee and thought about Fort Apache. He remembered how when it was over, and he could still see blood on his hands from the battles, he had thought he was no good for any woman, not ever.

Suddenly, there was a knock at the door.

Wes tensed, moving to the window and listening.

"Wes, let me in. It's Rio."

For a long moment, Wes hesitated. He leaned over the desk and slid the shutter just enough to see that Rio was alone. Making a quick judgment, he shoved the desk aside, removed the bar, and let the man inside as he drew his six-gun with his left hand.

"Put it away," Rio said. "I'm here to help."

"Where have you been?"

"I'd taken off a couple of days ago, headed for the Coast so I could get up to Juneau, but I ran into this fellow who was goin' to Butte for the marshal. He told me what was happenin', so I came back."

"Hollis and Haney are in the back room."

Rio turned to look at Cindy sleeping on the bunk. He and Wes moved the desk back in front of the door. Then Rio helped himself to some coffee while Wes filled him in.

Rio's buckskins were glowing yellow in the pale light as he listened in awe. He shook his head. "With that girl, why do you need us?"

Wes grinned and sipped his coffee. "Because she won't do what I tell her."

Rio chuckled. "Yeah, that's a problem with women, all right."

"Ain't it kinda late in the year to head for Alaska? By the time you get up there, the channel will be iced over."

Rio shrugged, fingering his cup. "Yeah, well, I got sick of the Grubers and had to go somewhere."

Wes glanced at the furniture heaped in front of the door. He stood up, peered out a window, and saw nothing but an empty, moonlit street. Then he sat down again to refill his cup. They talked about the old days for hours, then took turns sleeping and watching.

Just before dawn, they were both barely awake when they heard a sudden roar of hoofbeats and a loud clatter on the boardwalk. Wes leaped to his feet, drawing his six-gun with his left hand. Rio stood up slowly, almost lazily.

And then thunder struck the door as a huge pole came barreling through above the desk. Another pole struck the right window, shattering the shutters.

## Chapter Ten

Six-gun in his left hand, Wes stood frozen as the door and windows started caving in before their eyes. Cindy jumped up from the bunk, running for her Winchester.

Hollis and Haney came out. The rancher grabbed Cindy's arm and thrust her into the back room. She was so surprised, she didn't protest but held on to her rifle.

The men inside began to fire through the broken boards.

In the cells, the two prisoners cowered against the back wall, then dropped to their knees, worried stray bullets would hit them or the dynamite.

Gunfire from the inside of the jail did not deter the attackers, and the poles kept slamming through the walls and door. Someone was on the roof, stomping and trying to close the chimney. Rio fired up, but missed somehow, and the man kept stomping and tearing at the roof. Rio fired again. They heard a yell, then the sound of a body rolling off the roof.

Wes carefully picked up one of the sticks of dynamite, leaving the other in the bucket in front of the cells. He swallowed hard as he nervously edged around the shattering window to the right of the door. He had no fuses, and the old stick had nothing to light. He could only hope it was so volatile that it would explode on impact.

Now gunfire was being returned, and a bullet cut through Haney's shoulder. Hollis was stunned by a bullet in his side. Both men dropped to their knees, momentarily stunned. Rio knelt with them but kept firing at the cracks in the walls.

Cindy peered out of the back room and began firing over their heads, shells spitting out of her Winchester.

Wes suddenly jerked the broken shutter the rest of the way, took a deep breath, and threw the dynamite out into the early light. When it hit the ground in the middle of Gruber's men, Wes couldn't get a shot at it, but the crazed men didn't even see it and were about to stomp over it as they charged with the poles. He shoved the shutter in place, then dived for the floor as Rio pulled the other men down flat.

The dynamite exploded with a deafening roar. The impact shook the front of the jail violently and threw the wall inward, debris and boards and half the roof landing on everyone inside.

Outside, men were screeching and horses stampeding.

Wes shoved part of the wall off of him and got to his feet. He unbarred the broken door with Rio's help. With their six-guns in one hand and a rifle in the other, they charged out into the first light of day, each leaping to one side. They fired rapidly as the survivors staggered to their feet and fired back with fury.

Silas Gruber, bloodied and furious, was pulling himself up by the hitching rail, even as he turned his six-gun on Wes.

Hollis leaned out and shot Silas between the eyes, and the man spun around and fell back into the mud, face-down. Men were shooting blindly, crazily, while Wes and Rio fought back, stumbling over the fallen poles and ropes.

Then, just as suddenly, the gunfire stopped.

Men lay dead everywhere, and one wounded horse trotted away but seemed destined to survive.

Haney and Hollis, followed by Cindy, made their way onto the boardwalk to stand near Wes and Rio. Still carrying her Winchester, Cindy put her hand to her mouth and turned away from the sight of the dead. Haney and Hollis sank down on the nearly collapsed bench in front of the jail, while Rio walked around checking for life.

Wes stood alone in the doorway of the jail. He felt as if he could never kill another man. Down the street, he saw Churchill, Sellers, and Angela coming out of the café. Others were showing themselves. Doors were opening, curtains drawing back at the windows.

Wes bent down to pick up a dead man's six-gun just as a rifle cracked, the bullet whistling over his head and through the open door.

No one heard it hit the bucket in front of the cells.

A horrendous, deafening explosion sucked the roof and walls into a vacuum. Debris covered them and the inside of the jail. Boards and roof and windows spiraled down. Dust and smoke spun around them. The echo of the explosion was a long time dying.

Wes shoved the boards from his back and rose to one knee, staring across the street as a stunned Martha Gruber lowered her rifle. There was nothing left of the inside of the jail, nor of her sons.

He turned to pull Cindy from under the wall, her Winchester still clamped in her right hand. There was a bruise on her right cheek, and she was favoring her left leg. He helped Haney and Hollis stand. Then he turned to kneel and shove another part of the wall away from Rio, who was trying to get up.

He heard Martha's Winchester as the lever threw another shell in the chamber. Before he could look up, he heard a rifle crack. Martha gasped, firing toward Wes but missing as she fell forward, sprawling face-down and rolling over on her back with arms flailing. Then she lay still.

Surprised, Wes got to his feet and turned.

Cindy was slowly letting her Winchester slide from her grasp. She looked nauseated. He moved to her side and let her slide into his arms. She buried her face in his chest and sobbed; she had never killed a human being before.

As he held her shivering form, he looked into the street where the crowd was circling. He saw Churchill, Sellers, and Angela approaching, but he continued to hold Cindy, who had just saved his life.

Churchill was grim as he walked up to them. "You sure managed to get out of this one, Carson."

From up the street at the doctor's office, they could see Perryman being helped down the stairs. The lawman leaned on the doctor, barely able to walk.

Sellers came up, his arm around Angela. He looked pompous, as if he were in control. "Well, Carson, you're still alive."

Cindy moved away from Wes and made a face. "No thanks to either of you."

Angela straightened. "What do you mean?"

Cindy turned to Wes. "I saw Churchill and Sellers going to the livery where the Grubers were, and not long after that, an ambush was set for Mr. Hollis. I figure Sellers was bound and determined to have that whole ranch. Only trouble was, he didn't know Angela would be ridin' with them.''

Angela's face went white. ''Miss Taylor, that's a terrible thing to say.''

''She's jealous,'' Sellers said.

''But,'' Hollis said, ''I figure she's right.''

Sellers shook his head. ''You're wrong, Mr. Hollis. Why, Churchill and I went up there to try to talk Gruber out of this battle.''

''That's right,'' Churchill agreed, sweating.

''Wrong.'' Becker, the blacksmith, came out of the crowd. ''I heard Churchill and Sellers, both of 'em, through the livery barn, and I saw 'em through the cracks, but I was afraid to do anything about it. This whole town's been afraid of the Grubers, but now they're gone, and I figure it's time we stood up on our own two feet.''

Perryman had made it to the front of the jail. His eyes were wide with amazement. ''Carson, I don't think I'll be leavin' you in charge of my jail no more. As for you, Churchill, and you, Sellers, you're under arrest.''

Angela went to her father, who was bleeding and leaning on the debris. She put her arm around him as she stared at Sellers and Churchill being disarmed by Becker.

''You can lock 'em in my storeroom,'' a merchant said.

The crowd became friendlier, some towing away

the bodies from the scene. Sellers and Churchill were frantic.

"You're making a mistake," Sellers insisted. "I'll get a lawyer. I'll sue this town."

"I'm justice of the peace," Churchill protested.

"Yeah," Becker said, "but all you got to do now is worry if you're gonna fit in that storeroom."

The prisoners were led away, and Wes stood next to Cindy, his gaze meeting Angela's.

"Wes," Angela said, her eyes filled with tears, "it seems I've been wrong about everything. Can you forgive me?"

Cindy's gaze was fixed on Angela's flushed face as Wes nodded. He knew that Angela was free once more, but he couldn't react.

It was then that a wagon came in from the north and a rider from the south. Seated on the wagon seat was Clarisa Taylor and her father-in-law, Grandpa Taylor. Both stared in disbelief at the jail as Clarisa pulled the team to a halt.

Cindy limped over to the wagon.

The rider was Deputy U.S. Marshal Wiler, a huge man with big hands, a large nose, and an easy grin. He reined up, leaned on the pommel of his saddle, and asked, "You sure you need me around here?"

Clarisa swung down from the wagon and hugged Cindy. "We were so worried about you when you didn't come home yesterday." Then she looked at the wounded Haney and frowned. ''Mr. Haney, you're always in trouble.''

''I guess I need lookin' after,'' Haney said, then turned red at his words.

The doctor was ordering the wounded, including Wes, to his office. Cindy reluctantly picked up her Winchester and climbed into the wagon with her mother and grandfather, then sat looking at Wes's back as he walked with the other men. Tears filled her eyes, for now that the excitement was over, she was sick to her stomach and devastated by the carnage. Her mother hugged her.

It was only when Wes was at the foot of the stairs to the doctor's office that he realized Cindy was leaving. He waved to the Taylors as the wagon moved up the street, and Cindy twisted to wave back.

When the dust cleared in Shotgun Wells, Rio and Wes elected to help the marshal take the prisoners to Butte. Becker went along to testify, and the judge sentenced Churchill and Sellers to ten years in prison.

Meanwhile, the Army was planning to confiscate Gruber cattle, based on Wes's affidavit of what he had overheard.

From there, Rio wanted to go to Alaska, but at the local café in Butte, he began flirting with a chubby blond widow, who flirted back, and before Wes's eyes, Rio was planning his fifth marriage.

Heading south to Shotgun Wells by himself, Wes didn't know what to do. A woman he had loved so much her rejection had devastated him was now free. Another woman had fought at his side.

It was morning when he found himself riding over to the Hollis spread. Pete and Barney were at the corrals with Haney. The sun was bright and Haney was in his best shirt with a little string tie. He showed no signs of the head injury from the battle of Shotgun Wells.

"Haney's goin' courtin'," Pete said with a grin.

Haney rode out of the corral with Wes walking alongside. Then the foreman reined up and looked down at him. "Anything you want me to tell Cindy?" he asked.

"Yeah, I'll be there first light to take her on a picnic. Want to come along?"

"You do your own courtin'. I got my hands full."

"Mr. Hollis home?"

Haney nodded, and Wes went up to the fancy ranch house. Maria let him inside. He saw Angela and Hollis sitting together near the hearth.

Hollis stood up quickly, though he was still favoring his leg. "Wes, I'm glad to see you."

They shook hands, and Wes looked at Angela. So much had happened in the last five years and in the last five days, he felt as if they were a hundred miles apart.

"Angela's going back East," Hollis said as he

sat down. "Maybe you could convince her not to go."

Angela's face turned pink, but she leaned forward in her chair. "Yes, you could do that, Wes."

Wes felt his face burning. "I reckon maybe you'd be happier back there, Angela."

"So it's Cindy Taylor?" she asked.

He nodded with a lump in his throat he couldn't swallow, because he realized she was right.

She stood up slowly and walked to the foot of the stairs, then turned with a smile. "Don't worry about me, Wes. I left three beaus back there my last visit. And this time, I'll be more careful."

Knowing he had no choice but to let go of the past, he watched her go upstairs. Then he turned to Hollis, who looked disappointed.

Slowly Wes pulled the deed from inside his shirt. "Mr. Hollis, I'm returnin' this to you. I had no right to ask for it."

"Well, I don't want it back, Wes. You keep it, and I'll help you build. I'll even supply the timber. And when you're ready, you pick out them cows and heifers."

Wes hesitated, his noble gesture lost. "Sir, I don't figure it was right, askin' for that place."

"You listen to me, Wes. I lost both my sons, and my daughter's goin' back East to marry some other dude who knows which fork to use, 'counta that's what she likes. But me, this is my home, and I'm gonna get mighty lonesome. I'd sure take it kindly if you and your Cindy settled at Turkey Creek and invited me to Sunday dinner now and then, and that's about the longest speech I ever made.''

Wes grinned. ''Sunday dinner it is.''

''You asked her yet?''

''No, and it sure won't be easy.''

''She's a fiery one, all right.''

The next morning Wes showed up at the Taylor spread wearing a new shirt he had bought in Butte. Haney and Clarisa came out with Cindy, who was carrying a large basket and wearing her riding outfit. She looked wonderful.

Haney appeared foolish as all get out, and Clarisa was blushing. Grandpa Taylor was grinning from ear to ear, a happy man with romance blooming all around him.

''Glad you're here, Wes,'' Taylor said. ''I just can't handle that girl. Maybe you can do better.''

Cindy tried to be aloof, though her smile was bright. ''Wes Carson, next time you ask a girl on a picnic, come early.''

''I had to see Hollis.''

''And Angela?''

''She's goin' back East.''

Cindy smiled with pleasure. She handed him her basket, and then she mounted her mare. She rode on ahead, her hair flying in the wind. Wes followed, her basket bouncing on his saddle. Scotty trotted at their heels. Wes knew he was in for a hard time, but he was looking forward to it, and he smiled to himself.

Cindy suddenly turned, her eyes wide with excitement. "Mr. Haney asked my mother to marry him."

"She say yes?"

"Not yet, but she will. I guess she's just enjoying the courtin'."

"Women are like that, I reckon."

"Are you courtin' me, Wes Carson?"

He felt his face redden and burn. "I'm just takin' you on a picnic, Cindy Taylor."

She laughed nervously and rode on ahead.

They crossed the river and rode up into Turkey Creek, Scotty running on ahead. The sun was shining, the wind rising and cold, blowing Cindy's hair about her face. The grass was tall, green, and waving. The water in the busy creek spun with white foam. It was a wonderful world, Wes thought.

"I'll build up there," he said, nodding toward a knoll covered with wildflowers.

The first thing Scotty did was explore the area, especially a gully, but the dog didn't seem to find what he thought had been there. Then Scotty trotted along with Wes and Cindy, following the creek north.

When they dismounted on the knoll where Wes

would build a home, the dog went down to the creekbed. Wes set down the basket and tethered the horses on the flat.

He and Cindy lay back in the sweet grass, gazing up at the blue of the sky, and although they were two feet apart, he could feel her touch. His heart was pounding so loudly he feared she would hear it. A man couldn't be in a better spot than this, he thought.

He felt braver as he lay staring upward, watching a tiny drifting cloud, but his voice was wavering.

"Would you want to live here, Cindy?"

"What are you askin' me, Wes?"

His tongue was tangled. "Well, if I was to ask me to marry you, would I say yes?"

She giggled. "What?"

"I mean, if I was to ask you to marry me, would you say yes?"

"I don't know. Are you asking?"

He swallowed hard. This was a difficult woman. "Well, dad burn it, will you marry me?"

"That depends."

Frustrated, he rose on his elbow, and she rose on hers. They gazed at each other. Her smile was breathtaking.

"On what?" he asked.

"Whether you kiss me or not."

He reached for her, and she leaned toward him, her hair falling about her throat. He kissed her hard, and she giggled again. He had to laugh at her, because she was just not good at being coy. She was terribly nervous.

"Well?" he asked.

"Wes Carson, I knew I was going to marry you the day you rode into Shotgun Wells. When you pulled the Grubers off me and carried me on your horse, I was already designing my wedding dress."

He grinned and reached to kiss her again.

Suddenly, Scotty was biting at Wes's boot and grabbing his trousers. "Hey, I ain't wearin' spurs!"

"He's just playing."

"No, he's got somethin' in mind."

And Wes got up, pulling Cindy to her feet. They followed Scotty across the creek, stepping on big rocks, moving over the rushing water to the other side and toward the red cliff wall.

Within the hour, Scotty had led them to a pile of brush against the cliff, and the dog pawed at it. Wes pulled the brambles aside and rolled some big rocks away.

There, staring at them, was the opening to a mine. Dark and beckoning, it was about four feet high and as wide.

"Wes, do you know what this means?" Cindy asked. "Scotty was the prospector's dog."

"And he hated jingling spurs because that's what Simon and Sloan were wearing."

She knelt, tears in her eyes as she cuddled the frisky dog. "Oh, Scotty, I'm so sorry."

Wes shoved the rocks and brambles back in place and stood gazing at the spot. "Well, now we know where it is."

"What will you do, Wes?"

"Don't want no gold rush here. I'll talk to Mr. Hollis. He'll know what to do. And I reckon he's got some rights to a share of it."

Cindy stood up and gazed up at him with love shining in her eyes. "I adore you, Wes Carson."

Looking down at her, he knew a man couldn't ask for more. He felt his heart swell.

He drew her into his arms. Scotty began to tug at his trouser leg, growling and snarling but not tearing the cloth. A happy man, Wes lifted the squirming dog into their embrace, then turned his gaze toward the blue of the sky and murmured his thanks.

The maverick gun was about to be branded for life.